Boiling Shadow

Tim Mendees

MANNISON PRESS, LLC
FLORIDA | NEW YORK

Copyright © 2021 by Tim Mendees

All rights reserved. No part of this book may be reproduced or used in any manner without the express written permission of the publisher, except for brief quotations in a book review.

This is a work of fiction. Names, characters, businesses, places, events, and incidents are either the products of the author's imagination or used in a fictitious manner. Any resemblance to actual persons, living or dead, or actual events is purely coincidental.

First Edition 2021
Published by Mannison Press, LLC
ISBN: 9798753848338

Cover design by Deidre J Owen © 2021 | deidrejowen.com
Editing by Morgan Schafer at Mannison Press, LLC
Interior design by Deidre J Owen

Visit mannisonpress.com.

For Linda, Arthur Machen, and August Derleth,
without whom...

"All these are but dreams and shadows; the shadows that hide the real world from our eyes."

—Arthur Machen, *The Great God Pan*

Contents

Preface: A Catalogue of Injuries — i

Part I: Broken Timber and Torn Flesh — 3

Part II: The Tree and The Shadow — 41

Part III: Blood and Glass — 91

Part IV: Fire and Revelation — 139

Acknowledgements — 197

About the Author — 199

A Catalogue of Injuries

PREFACE BY TIM MENDEES

Welcome back to Hollowhills. I hope you enjoy your stay.

What you hold in your grubby mitts is both a sequel and prequel to my first solo release, Burning Reflection. It is also the latest entry into the ongoing saga of the isolated Cornish village of Hollowhills. A sub mythos in my overall mythos. It sounds more confusing than it actually is.

When I started concocting my odd little tales, I did what many aspiring writers of cosmic horror do, I tried to ape H.P. Lovecraft's style and settings. My first attempts were set in what is known as Lovecraft Country and were about as authentic as Japanese Scotch whiskey. I have never set foot in New England, so I didn't have a clue what I was wittering on about. Feeling deflated at my faltering attempts, I retired to my bedroom with a good book and prepared to sulk.

As serendipity would have it, I had just received the special collector's edition of Ramsey Campbell's The Inhabitant of the Lake through the mail. His first collection and still his most Cthulhu Mythos-tastic creation. Amongst the bonus material is a series of letters between the Liverpudlian author and the head honcho of Arkham House and member of the original Lovecraft Circle, Mr August Derleth.

Campbell had done the exact same thing that I had with similar results. All of the tales in his manuscript were set in Arkham, Dunwich, Innsmouth, etc. Derleth liked what he read and was only too happy to publish... on one condition. That Campbell went away and create his own milieu. Quite rightly, Derleth gave him the advice that would help him become one of Britain's finest ever horror writers. Basically, he was told to write what he knew. The best advice ever given to a green writer. This was the turning point not only for Mr. Campbell, but for me also. I honestly hope there is some kind of afterlife where I can buy Mr. Derleth a pint!

A lightbulb went off over my head. I needed somewhere with similar qualities to Lovecraft's Massachusetts or Campbell's Severn Valley. It had to be steeped in antiquity, isolated, wild, and a place of dark legend. It didn't take me more than five minutes to settle on Cornwall. With its fishermen's tales, miner superstitions, and links to various British myths and legends, it seemed like the perfect place for me to set up shop, so to speak.

As a child, I had been taken on a family holiday down to Cornwall which included a visit to Poldark Mine. It is an experience that will never leave me. I was both excited and terrified by the sheer scale of it. You could honestly believe while standing on a high gantry looking down that you could get to the centre of the Earth if you decided to jump. So, when I created my fictional corner of Cornwall, I knew I needed a mining town.

If Betyls Cove is my Arkham, then Hollowhills is my Dunwich. An isolated mining village in the wilds of Bodmin Moor. It first appeared in the story "The Hollow Hills" which was my take on the themes of one of my favourite authors, Arthur Machen. Funnily enough, it was Machen who influenced Lovecraft in the first place. The Great God Pan is a noticeable influence on The Dunwich Horror and several more of his rural nightmares. It's nice to bring the influence of the 'Welsh Wizard' back to the British Isles.

Needless to say, I fell in love with the rotting, twisted place, so it was no surprise that I returned there pretty quickly. The very next thing I wrote after "The Hollow Hills" was Burning Reflection. Originally meant to be a short story, it became a novella when I realised that I was already two thousand words over the upper limit and not even halfway through. That, dear reader, is the story of my writing career. Still, I crossed my fingers that I would find it a home and kept going. I was overjoyed when Mannison Press agreed to publish it and absolutely blown away by the positive response it received. Eagle-eyed readers may have noticed that the sinister B&B featured in "The Hollow Hills" is none other than the Lester House... Retconning at its most insidious.

While I was writing *Burning Reflection*, I had the ideas that would become the book you have in your hands. I had pretty much a full outline for this and a, as yet unwritten, third novella before I had finished it. I knew what characters I wanted to spare, which to kill, and where it was all going. There is also another story, "Afterimage" that is a present-day pseudo-sequel to *Burning Reflection* and another, as yet unpublished, short that further adds to the overall story and acts as a prequel to "The Hollow Hills." That's not to say that you can't enjoy this tale without reading all the other stuff, because you can. One of my aims was to make it both standalone and part of a series. I hope I have succeeded.

Before I let you dive on in, I just wanted to tell you about how it came about:

Throughout my life, I have had several significant injuries, some of which are experienced by our hapless protagonist. Yep, everything that happens to Bill has, at one point or another, happened to me. Some of the situations have been tweaked slightly for narrative purposes, but they are as close as possible. I'm not going to spoiler you, but I hope that knowledge adds to the wince factor. I have the scars to prove each and every incident.

I first intended to call this novella "A Catalogue of Injuries" and aimed to add some more of my more painful experiences. Alas, I couldn't work motorcycle accidents, a cabinet speaker falling on my face, or having my feet deep-fried into a Victorian narrative. Probably for the best. I also initially wrote the first part in the first person. I'm glad I changed my mind. It has turned out so much better this way. I can never think of a way to end first-person stories believably. This is an issue in cosmic horror, a genre where the protagonist usually ends up dead or insane.

Finally, I will stop wittering on and let you begin. Whether it is your first visit to Hollowhills or if you are a veteran of its horrors, I hope you enjoy your stay and hope to see you again when I write the third and final part of the saga.

Tim Mendees

15/10/2021

Both "The Hollow Hills" and "Afterimage" can be found in the short story collection *The Pseudopod That Rocks the Cradle* (Mannison Press, 2021).

~I~

Broken Timber and Torn Flesh

WILLIAM JOHNSON PEERED OUT OF THE WINDOW and sighed as the weather-beaten Clarence carriage came to a rattling stop outside his grandfather's home. This was the last place on Earth he wanted to be on a bright Saturday in July. When the morning light had streamed through the window of his airy room at his parent's home in Truro that morning, he had been filled with joy at the thought of going for a pleasure jaunt. His governess Viola's appearance at his bedroom door wearing a summer coat and hat had practically confirmed his suspicions. Sadly, they were wrong.

Two stout Hackney horses had little difficulty conveying his young body and the slight frame of his governess out of the only town he had ever known. Viola was fresh-faced with a delicate, almost bird-like bone structure and it was her demeanour that indicated to William that all was far from well. Throughout the journey, she was withdrawn and so far removed from her usual cheery self that William was in no doubt that something was amiss. Her eyes were red and puffy and had lost their jocular twinkle that he relied upon to get him through those long months when his parents were abroad.

As a merchant of high standing, William's father was often called upon to attend trade talks in far-flung places, leaving Viola as his rock; in fact, he almost saw her as his big sister. Seeing such a strong, steady figure in his life wilt and droop like some sickly bloom filled him with a kind of tangible dread that only deepened the further they travelled into the bleak and inhospitable countryside.

Every time William asked her what was wrong, Viola would smile wanly and affect an air of jollity before assuring him that everything was fine. Sure, he was young, but not so young that he couldn't tell that she was lying. As a consequence, after an hour or so of morose silence, he was starting to become fractious. The more she tried to change the subject, with faux enthusiasm about rocks and wind-battered trees, the more anxious and irritable he became.

William had only visited his grandfather at his Hollowhills home a handful of times in the past due to some kind of acrimony between him and William's father. Their contretemps had reportedly started after William's father had decided not to follow in *his* father's footsteps, insisting instead on carving out his own path in the world. George Johnson was the proud owner of the largest tin mine in the Hollowhills area and expected his son and heir to take up the reins as he increased in years. Walter Johnson had other ideas, and wanted a career that would let him see the world, the last thing he wanted was to be trapped in Hollowhills for the rest of his life.

The most vivid memory that William had of his grandfather was of a strong and taciturn man with fists like shovels wolfing down a Sunday dinner like it was his last. They had rarely spoken to each other during his last visit, but then, George didn't really talk to anyone, truth be told. After all, he had just buried his beloved wife, Marjory. William's grandmother had been a lovely little woman who perfectly balanced out his grandfather's gruffness with a cheery personality and warm smile. Unfortunately, she had developed a wasting disease and withered away before George's eyes. He was never the same man after that.

Opening the door of the conveyance, William was struck by how overgrown the gardens had become in the intervening years. Ivy had crept across the facade like a rash, nearly engulfing the doorway. The last time he had been here, the flowerbeds had been bright and vibrant, now they were a dull tangle of weeds and feral herbs. Even the windows looked neglected; they were muddy with rain streaks and peppered with bird droppings.

Stepping down from the cab, William managed to avoid the large patch of mud at the end of the path. Viola wasn't so lucky, however, and ended up with sticky mud on the hem of her dress. As you can imagine, he found this hysterical, which finally broke the tension between the two somewhat. This brief moment of levity was shattered the moment his grandfather's maid, Iris, opened the door. She was often a dour character but on that day she was wearing the sort of expression that you would have expected from a constipated goat.

"Come in, Master William," Iris crooned, her voice as brittle as shards of broken glass. "Your grandfather is waiting for you in the library." Iris pointed to a door next to the grand staircase that wound up to the first-floor landing. "Leave your suitcase here. Viola and I will take care of it."

"Thank you, Iris," William squeaked like a startled church mouse. Just when the day couldn't get any more unnerving, he was invited into an area of the house that had always been strictly off limits—his grandfather's library.

Wandering through the draughty hall with a powerful smell of polish tickling his nostrils, William gazed up at the sombre portraits of hardy-looking ancestors that lined the sweeping staircase up to the first-floor landing. Looking back towards the door, he saw Iris take Viola aside. Both women were shaking their heads and wringing their hands like distressed washerwomen. It was so out of character for both parties that William's heart was in his mouth by the time he reached the heavy door to the library. He gave it a polite knock before hesitantly grasping the polished brass knob and pushing the door ajar.

Seeing the library for the first time, William could fully understand his grandfather's reluctance to let him inside. It was set on two levels with a high ceiling and a grand chandelier in the centre. From floor to ceiling on the three covered walls were hundreds of meticulously arranged books with exquisite leather bindings. William's father had explained that his grandfather was very protective of his books and, due to William's age and the opportunity for mischief, he couldn't risk his grubby little paws touching his prized possessions. All perfectly reasonable, of course, but at the time, William had been peeved. As soon as you tell a child that he can't go somewhere, that is the only place he will desire to go. Children have more in common with cats than most people think.

In the centre of the room sat a series of grand leather seats, an antique globe, a drinks trolley, and a huge mahogany desk piled with books, papers, and various writing paraphernalia. George sat hunched behind the desk like a large, squat toad. He was holding a letter in his hand, his eyes were intensely focused on the words and his hands trembled perceptibly.

George hadn't noticed his arrival, so William cleared his throat politely. "*Ahem*, hello, Grandfather. You wanted to see me?"

"What?" George barked, peering over the top of his half-moon spectacles. After a second, the glaze left his eyes and he forced a smile. "Yes! Come on in, my boy, sit down." He indicated a quilted Georgian chair next to the desk with a tilted hand. "Now, young man, do you prefer William or Bill?"

This was something his grandson had never before considered. His parents, on their infrequent visits home, had always called him "William." "Bill." He smiled after a moment's consideration, it sounded much more grownup than "William," and he hated "Willy" with a passion that bordered on the neurotic.

"Good choice, my lad." George beamed. "Bill is a good, strong name. William sounds a bit toffee-nosed if you ask me, like that poet chap, Blake." Despite owning many volumes of poetry, George had little time for the arts. "Now, Bill." He folded his massive hands on the desk in front of him and exhaled deeply, puffing out his bewhiskered cheeks. "I have some very bad news, I'm afraid. You see, there has been an accident..."

George proceeded to inform William that both of his parents had perished in a shipwreck along the coast near Betyls Cove. It was a sad fact that George's bedside manner left a lot to be desired. He just kind of blurted it out without any preamble to soften the blow. It hit Bill like a prized pugilist. He wailed, sobbed, and shook uncontrollably. George didn't have the first idea of how to console a distraught child, so he called for Viola. She trotted into the library and wrapped Bill in her arms as he balled his little heart out. Once he'd recovered enough to speak,

Bill looked up to find that his grandfather had vanished. He didn't see him again until supper.

At the time, Bill had taken George's disappearance as him not caring, which got them off on the wrong foot somewhat. He later realised that his relative had taken himself off down to the garden to grieve in private. As a mine owner and a product of his generation, it simply wasn't the "done" thing to show any sign of weakness, even to family. He had spent his life cultivating an image of strong-minded efficiency and he couldn't afford to lose it at this late stage. He quickly made it up to his grandson, but at the time Bill was furious.

Bill hardly slept a wink that night. The creak of the ancient roof timbers as the wind pummeled the coast made him imagine a wide range of spooks and spectres that in retrospect could have been seen as a warning. The one time that Bill did manage to drift off, he was troubled by an intense nightmare.

♆♃♄♇

Awakening in a dream, Bill gazed through thick fog at the hazy light from the nearby lighthouse. The keeper sounded the horn at regularly spaced intervals, sending vibrations through the cliffs and causing roosting seabirds to flee in terror. Wild waves slammed the rocks below with such force that he nearly lost his footing and tumbled to a watery grave. Looking around, Bill could barely see the path that led down towards the dim shadows of a town below. Everything was bathed in a lambent glow from the bloated moon that hung low above the sea.

In the distance, he could hear the creak of stressed timbers as a ship struggled against the swell of the tide. The air was suddenly filled with the sounds of clattering bells and panicked screams. On the beach below, several men carrying oil lamps raced towards the crag. Peering towards the source of the sound, he saw smudges of light becoming visible as a ship raced towards the craggy promontory.

With a colossal crash, the off-course vessel struck the jagged rocks. That hellish din was followed by a tremendous roar of cracking timber and twisting metal as the ship was rent asunder. The awful cries of the doomed passengers rose to a crescendo that made Bill's bones ache and his teeth itch. As tears rolled down his adolescent cheeks, the cries were mercifully cut off by water rushing into their lungs.

"Ahoy!" the men on the beach cried as the ship was swallowed by the sea. "Any survivors?"

Racing to the edge of the promontory, Bill fell to his knees and gazed over the edge in a desperate attempt to spy anyone still clinging onto life. Alas, there was nothing. All he could discern under the swirling miasma were splinters of wood and fabric twisting like ghostly jellyfish. After a while, the sounds of the search party ceased as they gave up hope and went back to the safety of the lighthouse. Bill was left alone, shivering with cold and shock, with only the mournful sound of the foghorn for company. Raising himself off the damp grass, whispering a silent prayer for the lost, Bill slowly turned…

"William…"

His heart nearly imploded as a gurgling whisper called to him from the fog. It was familiar but *different* at the same time. "Mother?" he asked softly and, when no answer came, started to walk hesitantly towards the source of the sound.

"Over here…"

This time, the awfully distorted voice came from further over and was male. "Father?" Bill's slippered feet scuffled in the sunbaked scrub as he quickened his pace and hurried forwards. "Mother, Father, where are you…where are you?!"

The echoing clatter of a kicked stone bouncing off the rocks alerted Bill to imminent danger. He pulled up sharply and looked down. He had been mere inches away from hurtling off the headland to the shingle below. As he panted for breath, an unknown voice chuckled in a deep timbre.

"Come closer…"

"You're not my parents! Who are you?" Bill screamed into the fog hysterically as he backed slowly away from the edge and collided with a figure.

He didn't want to turn around, but knew that he must. The figure felt rigid against his back and seawater soaked through his nightshirt to his goosefleshed skin. Slowly, holding his breath, he turned.

"Hello, William…"

A Piercing scream that Bill never knew he was capable of escaped from his trembling lips as he took in the shape before him. It was his mother…and she was dead. Half of her once pretty face was a mangled mess of necrotic flesh and shattered bone. Her eyeball dangled obscenely, almost touching her blue lips. Cackling maniacally, she reached out for him with elongated fingers tipped with savage nails. Ducking sideways, Bill dodged her touch as she started to laugh with the voice of the unknown man.

Bill turned and ran. He ran as fast as his frozen legs would allow. He had never excelled at physical activity, but at that point, he could have outpaced England's first eleven. Following the track down from the outcrop, his feet slipped on the shingle and he barely avoided landing flat on his face. Risking a glance behind him, Bill was shocked to see that the cadaverous image of his drowned mother had been replaced by a patch of inky blackness that stood in sharp contrast to the moonlit fog.

Baleful orange eyes like hot coals snapped open at head height on the amorphous thing as it began to form itself into a roughly humanoid shape. From all around, the grim cackle of his pursuer drowned out the crash of the waves and the blasts from the foghorn until Bill's ears were filled with its insidious rattle.

"Bill… Will… William… Willy… Come to me."

Screaming at the top of his lungs, the terrified boy found himself completely incapable of flight as the shape shuddered towards him. Each step the shadow took caused its edges to become jagged and barbed like it was wrapped in Hawthorne. It was mere inches from engulfing him when he was spun around and shaken violently by the bloated and drowned spectre of his father.

"You are in great danger. Don't let the shadow taste your blood!"

Bill screamed as the spectre threw him headfirst into a dense patch of fog.

♌♌♌♌

Waking in a cold sweat, screaming himself hoarse, Bill sat bolt upright and scanned the room with fear widened eyes. The room seemed to shudder and relax around him as though the house itself had just exhaled after sucking all of the oxygen from the room. The sheets were tangled around his feet, causing him to tumble to the floor with a *thud* as he tried to stand. Bill was a sniveling wreck with eyes streaming with tears as salty as the waves in his nightmare.

Struggling to breathe, relief washed over him as the door swung open and Viola entered carrying a blooming Davy lamp. She placed it on the chest of drawers next to the door and rushed to his aid. As she cooed gently that everything was alright, the awful images of his deceased parents' faces flashed before his eyes, reminding him that things most assuredly weren't.

She held Bill tightly while rocking back and forth and they quietly wept together.

Viola Smith had joined the Johnson household as a girl of sixteen and had quickly become part of the family. She had looked after William since he was old enough to walk and, if truth be told, was closer to his parents than he would ever be. In many ways, she was more of a big sister than a governess and the tragic passing of her employers had left her devastated. After sharing their sorrow for a while, she tucked Bill into bed and returned to her room down the corridor.

Bill didn't sleep another wink that evening; instead, he sat and watched the ferocious winds batter the garden from his rattling sash-window. Time passed quickly as he lost himself in the hypnotic dance of the various trees and shrubs. At some point, he had retrieved his sketchbook and started to draw the scene below him. As the sun rose, the winds subsided and a refreshing air of calm fell over the house. It was only as the warm sunlight fell over his body that his muscles finally relaxed.

Knock, knock

"Good morning, William," Viola called out as she opened the door. "Did you manage to get some sleep?"

Bill shrugged. "No, I couldn't settle. And it's Bill now."

"Pardon?"

"Bill. My name is Bill now. Mother called me William."

Viola smiled weakly. She looked as though she hadn't slept a wink either. Red and black smudges ringed her bright green eyes and her cheeks were pale as milk. "Very well, Bill it is." She walked over to the bed and started to straighten the sheets. Once it was correct, she turned her attention to Bill's drawing. "What's that?" she asked, pointing to a dark shape between the trees that surrounded the entrance to the top garden at the far end of the property.

Bill had no recollection of drawing what looked like a man lurking on the boundary. He shook his head and shrugged. "Um… Nothing. It's just a shadow."

Ruffling his unruly brown hair, she straightened up and forced another smile. "Breakfast will be served in half an hour, cook says. We will be having it in the kitchen."

Bill's face creased in puzzlement. "Why not the dining room?"

Viola sighed. "Your grandfather is doing some renovations. It's like a building site in there. Didn't you think it was funny that we ate supper in the kitchen?"

In truth, the thought hadn't crossed his mind. "No, I…I wasn't myself last night."

Her face became a mask of sympathy as she squeezed his hand gently.

Before she could speak, Bill sniffed and said brightly, "Right, I'll be down shortly, I'll just get dressed."

"Very good. Then later we can go over your arithmetic."

She had said this with such enthusiasm that Bill instantly felt guilty for the grimace that spread across his face. He hated numbers; letters were fine, but numbers… Viola took his displeasure with good grace and tutted playfully as she left the room.

While Viola made her way back downstairs, Bill stared at the picture in puzzlement. He had scribble-shaded the shadow in such a way that it appeared to have the same harsh outline as the spectre in his dream. A cold chill traced its way down his spine as he raised his eyes and stared down at the garden. Everything was still, eerily so. After a moment's scrutiny, he snatched up the paper in his hands, screwed it up tightly, then tossed it under the bed. Out of sight, out of mind.

♎ ♍ ♌ ♋ ♊

Breakfast was nothing short of a triumph. Susan, the cook, had excelled herself. Plump butcher's sausages, crisp streaky bacon, and black pudding were accompanied by fried tomatoes and mushrooms topped with freshly laid eggs from the chickens in the yard adjacent to the barn. Bill struggled to complete his gargantuan repast and could only marvel as George wolfed his down in record time. By the Saints, that man could eat. Bill remembered his father once joking that he wasn't convinced that George didn't have a particularly ravenous tapeworm making a nest inside his bulbous belly.

George seemed much brighter that morning, wherever he had taken himself off to the previous afternoon, it had seemingly done him the world of good. He was garrulous and engaging. Unfortunately, Bill wasn't quite ready to forgive him just yet. He was still upset that he had seemingly abandoned him in his hour of need. It was only two days later when Bill discovered him crying buckets in the library, that he came to realise that he hadn't been heartless, it was just his way of dealing with things. That was when anger turned to pity for the old devil. Not only had he lost his wife, but his only son as well. Bill was all he had left.

Once he had stuffed his face, George excused himself by explaining that he had urgent business at the mine to take care of. He donned his stout boots, greatcoat, and flat cap then strolled off onto the moors. Bill was left with Viola and Iris sitting opposite each other, nibbling toast like a pair of dainty hens. Both of them were withdrawn and quite obviously mourning, which did little for his own mood. He couldn't cope with anyone else's sorrow on top of his own.

So, to break out of the oppressive vacuum, he offered to help Susan with the dishes. He wouldn't be doing that again in a hurry.

"Oh, Master Bill, that would be luvvly," she simpered in her warm Cornish burr. "Me back's playin' up somethin' chronic." With a wink to Iris that Bill failed to catch, she hobbled over to the table and sat down.

Bill was too fuzzy-headed to notice her deception, the woman was as fit as a ferret despite her age, and he set about playing the white knight.

Susan was one of those homey cooks that absolutely had to use every single knife, pot, plate, and utensil in the kitchen to simply boil an egg. The crafty old duck quickly took advantage of Bill's offer of help and set him to work scrubbing the cast-iron skillet. He would later become very fond of Susan, but at that moment in time, however, he could have bashed her over the head with her own rolling pin. At least his irritation went some way towards restoring Viola's smile. It appeared that even sorrow couldn't dampen the delights of *schadenfreude*.

Once the kitchen had been scrubbed to near oblivion and Bill was soaked to the skin and thoroughly peeved, he took up his sketchbook and set out to explore the house that, he had been informed as he hungrily munched on a sausage, was to be his home for the time being. Of course, his first port of call was the ruined dining room.

♎♋♉♓

Viola hadn't been exaggerating when she said that the once-sumptuous dining room now resembled a building site. The carpets had been ripped up and piled in a corner, and the oak-panel wainscoting had been removed and stacked, revealing rising damp on the external-facing wall. It was the discovery of this thick, black mould while hanging a picture of his beloved mine that had spurred George into action. Bill stood and took in the devastation around him and grinned.

When you are a child, there is something strangely exciting about renovation work. It may stem from the fact that you only really see the potential of the room without having a concept of the backbreaking work that it would entail. Bill wasn't yet old enough to connect the dots that reveal that improvement equals hard labour.

Bill's favourite part of this room had always been the fireplace. It was nothing grand, by the standards of the era, but had a kind of solid beauty that he was delighted to see remained. The slate hearth and stonework were still intact with the only difference being that a new oak mantelpiece had replaced the old one that had become marked by the presence of heavy ornaments and ingrained with dust over time.

As Bill moved towards the fireplace, he was struck by a feeling of curiosity. The walls had been painted in peacock green that had faded over the decades, yet above the fireplace was a rectangular patch that remained as vibrant as if it had been painted yesterday. It looked as though a picture had until recently hung there, but strangely, he had no recollection of a picture having been there on any of his previous visits.

Approaching the mysterious patch of bright paint, the light from the sagging bay window caught the hearth in such a way that it seemed to reveal a strange pattern in the centre slate. In a second, the clouds shifted and the illusion was dispelled. Bill had always been inquisitive and found himself titillated by the prospect of a mystery. Crouching down, he ran his hand from one end of the hearth to the other, the slates were perfectly flat apart from an odd roughness to the one in the centre. Tracing it with his finger, it appeared that there was some kind of etching there that was invisible to the naked eye.

Something about the pattern that had briefly revealed itself sent prickles of unease up and down the backs of his legs. It was almost as though a window had briefly opened onto some great and tantalising secret. Taking his sketchbook from under his arm, Bill tore out a pristine white page and laid it over the central portion of the hearth. Selecting a thick stick of charcoal from his drawing tin, he started at the topmost corner and commenced rubbing. As he surmised, the outer portions were flat, but as he moved to the centre, a series of lines started to appear.

There could have been no accident or simple quirk of geology that could have explained the otherwise unseen symbol that emerged as Bill brought the charcoal back and forth vigorously across the paper. Though he had only uncovered the uppermost tip of the design, it was clear that it was a symbol of some kind. It seemed to depict the tip of a series of interlinked star-like shapes and as he moved slowly down the page, a strange design, almost like an oddly warped Eye of Horus, started to become visible in the centre of the lines.

Hunched over, with one hand flat to steady the paper, Bill continued to rub. His eyes widened as more and more of the sinister design became visible. He was so absorbed in his task that he had no time to prepare for what happened next. Without warning, a forceful gale slammed the room from directly behind the chimney breast. Time seemed to slow to a crawl as the mantelpiece fell from its setting and slammed down upon the outstretched pinkie finger of his left hand with a mighty *bang!*

A curious thing about pain is that, sometimes, it is so sudden and so immense that the brain doesn't register it at first. It was only as Bill saw the bright red blood spreading across the white page that he realised that anything was wrong. Drawing his hand slowly back, his body went into an acute state of shock as a chunk of mangled skin, meat, and nail came away from the bloody stump of his finger. It was then that he started to scream.

As if in response, the windows started to rattle, the old and warped timbers clattering against the filthy glass panes. A dark shadow fell across the house, eclipsing the sunlight as Bill hugged his injured hand tightly to his stomach and doubling over as pain finally began to take hold. Tears flooded from his eyes, falling to the floor and making filthy clumps of dust on the bare boards. As his panic grew, an awful rattling moan that made his breath catch in the back of his throat burst from the gaping mouth of the chimney. For a moment, he was utterly paralysed, shaking and swaying on his knees before the star-shaped design that had been completed by rivulets of his brightly-coloured blood. It burned into his vision, seared onto his retinas like some awful afterimage of a photographed atrocity.

Bill's vision started to blur and grow dim as he fought to take air into his lungs. It felt as though not only was his precious blood leaving his body, but his very essence as well. As he hovered on the brink of oblivion, the door swung open with a *crash* as Iris rushed into the room. "My God in Heaven!" she screeched, then flew across the room and wrapped Bill in her spindly yet powerful arms. "Viola! Come quickly! Viola?"

As soon as Iris touched his skin, Bill gasped as though *something* had finally released his windpipe from a claw-like grip. Oxygen flooded his body, making him feel lightheaded and weightless.

Viola soon appeared in the doorway and shrieked in horror at the gory scene in front of her. "What the devil has happened?"

"His finger...we need to stop the bleeding." Iris was remarkably calm in stark contrast to her much younger counterpart.

Viola stood with her mouth agape and her hands raised to her chin.

"Don't just stand there dithering, Viola!" Iris snapped. "Pass me something to tie a tourniquet. Come on, be quick about it!"

Snapping out of her funk, Viola pulled a handkerchief from her pocket and waved it in the air. "Will this do?"

"Yes, yes. Now, go and fetch Dr. Lester. He lives in the cottage just past the inn." As Iris set about yanking Bill's arm in the air and tying the hankie tightly around the knuckle, Viola rushed from the room and out the front door flapping her arms at her sides like a startled sparrow.

Bill's hearing had been greatly impaired by a ferocious buzzing that brought to mind an angry swarm of bees trapped in a drainpipe. As a consequence, he'd caught only snippets of their conversation. His head throbbed and pulsed as his eyes reverberated with the pitch of the hellish din. Shadows and shapes started to form at the edges of his peripheral vision, crawling and creeping inwards towards his stricken form. The buzzing built into a rattle, then from a rattle to a roar.

As the pressure in Bill's head built towards the point of explosion, his mouth fell open and a slew of guttural syllables flowed out into the dusty air. "Hup n'ghftnahh h' nog ahfhtagnor!" His body fell limp and he sagged into Iris' arms.

"Bill? Bill…?" Iris gently fluttered his cheek with her left hand as his eyes rolled and his tongue lolled from the corner of his mouth.

"Good Lord!" Dr. Lester exclaimed as he swept into the room. Passing his top hat and cane to Viola who scurried behind him, he dropped to his knees and opened his leather Gladstone bag. "He's in shock. Hold him steady, Iris."

"Yes, Doctor. What's that?" she asked, nodding towards the brown bottle he took from his bag.

"Morphine. It'll calm him and kill the pain," Lester replied as he screwed a needle into the tip of a metal hypodermic syringe and filled it from the bottle.

"Oh!" Iris yelped. "Isn't that dangerous? I don't think Master George would approve."

Lester jumped like a scolded dog. "He's not here, is he?"

"No, he's down the pit."

"Good. We don't want any *unpleasantness*, do we?" Lester smiled as he pricked the syringe into Bill's skin. "Hold him steady now. It'll be all over soon."

The last thing Bill saw before drifting into a drugged sleep was a jagged shadow rising up behind Dr. Lester.

♎︎♍︎♎︎

Dr. Lester did a marvelous job of stemming the bleeding and sewing Bill back up. He was able to save roughly half of the top section of his patient's finger, but it would forever be much shorter than its opposite digit and almost triangular in shape. Once he had finished, he helped the ladies get Bill into bed and left Viola in charge. She was given a bottle of laudanum to help alleviate any pain Bill may encounter. Lester then made a speedy getaway before the man of the house returned.

When Bill awakened from his opiate slumber, the first thing that he was aware of was a foul odour. The horrid mixture of the iron tang of blood, the sharp bite of alcohol, and the stench of charred flesh hung over the bed like a shroud. Spectres of the opium clung to the corners and peeked out from behind the curtains as he struggled to rouse himself. For a blissful moment, Bill had completely forgotten the severing of the tip of his finger, but as the drug faded, the pain and the image of his mangled flesh returned. Bill gasped, making a shape next to the bed jump in surprise.

"Oh!" Viola exclaimed. "You're awake." Ever the dutiful guardian, she had been dozing in the chair next to the bed. "Here, drink some water."

Bill took the proffered glass and instantly tipped its contents all over the sheets. His hands were shaking like a goose at Christmas. "Sorry," he slurred. "I think I got you wet."

"Not to worry. A bit of water won't hurt me. I'm not a witch." She smiled as she retrieved a flannel off the table and started to mop herself down. "Now, let's try that again, shall we?" She only filled the glass halfway this time before once again handing it to Bill.

This time, he succeeded in bringing it to his lips. It tasted cool and refreshing. "Thank you," he croaked as he handed her back the glass.

"Now, how are you feeling? Groggy, no doubt?" She stopped fussing over the spillage for a second and placed her hand on his forehead. "Good, your temperature is returning to normal. You were burning up there for a while. Not to worry, I must assume that it was to do with Dr. Lester's medicine."

"I...I don't remember..." Words wouldn't come easily; his tongue felt like a wet towel slurping around in his mouth. It didn't help that his teeth were still numb. "What happened after?"

"The doctor stitched you up and we put you to bed. You've been out for hours. A proper little Rip Van Winkle, and no mistake."

It was then that Bill remembered the extent of his injuries. Pulling his injured hand out from under the covers, expecting the worst, it came as something of a disappointment to find it expertly bandaged. He wanted to gaze at his own torn flesh—such morbid creatures, children. "Will it scar?"

"I should think so, yes. You have lost the top of your finger. The doctor tried to sew it back on, but it was too badly damaged."

Bill frowned as he tried to measure the difference between the two fingers. It looked like he'd lost about two-thirds of an inch. "Oh..." he muttered despondently. In all the literature he had read, heroes were described as perfect creatures. Strong, handsome, and flawless. You never read of a dashing hero missing a quarter of a pinkie finger. Even if you did, it would have come from a heroic swordfight and not from a stupid accident.

Viola must have sensed his unease; she was always very perceptive. "Not to worry, you'll be the talk of the school. Children wear scars like badges of honour, especially in places like this, you'll see!"

This cheered him somewhat, but his spirits were quickly dampened again by a sudden realisation. "School?"

"Yes, Master George has got you a place at the schoolhouse in the village. That's good news, isn't it?"

"Yeah, I suppose." Bill sighed, sounding unconvinced. He liked the school in Truro and had friends there. What upset him the most, however, was the realisation of what this turn of events signified—he was indeed staying in that draughty old house and isolated village for the foreseeable future.

"Oh, I'm sure you will fit right in. Iris tells me that your father went there when he was your age. Now, you should try and get some more rest. I'll go and inform your grandfather that you are awake. He insisted on being kept informed." She stood and started towards the door before stopping and whispering conspiratorially, "Don't mention that Dr. Lester came *inside*, there's a dear."

"Why not?"

"I'm not quite sure." Viola shrugged. "I'll have to ask Iris. All I know is, he and your grandfather had a *falling out* about something. It won't do his blood pressure any good to know that he was in the house. Just don't mention it until Iris has had a chance to break it to him gently. Promise?"

Bill nodded silently. He was far too delirious to question her any further.

"Good. Now, you get some rest, you hear?"

Once Viola had departed, Bill looked once more at his bandaged hand before pulling the covers up to his chin, closing his eyes and surrendering to the pull of the morphine.

♎︎♏︎♌︎♍︎

Bang! Bang! Bang!

As the first light of dawn filtered in through the crack in the moth-eaten brocade curtains, Bill was startled awake by a hellish racket from downstairs.

Each slam of metal on stone sent shockwaves through his body, terminating in a painful throb in the tip of his injured finger. Disorientated and bleary eyed, he wobbled out of bed and threw his dressing gown over his striped pyjamas.

The residual morphine had turned his knees to jelly, making Bill's walk to the bedroom door something of a strange experience. The floor seemed too hard and his body too heavy. Another series of heavy bangs banished the cobwebs a little as the metallic tang of adrenaline appeared at the back of his tongue.

Stepping onto the landing and shuffling to the stairs, Bill caught Susan's eye as she staggered in the front door hefting a sack of spuds. "Morning, Susan, what's going on?"

Susan shrugged and tutted before nodding towards the dining room. "Lord alone knows… ee's got a ruddy bee in 'is bonnet again."

As the much put-upon cook shuffled off towards the kitchen, Bill started to make his way down the sweeping staircase. Glancing up at the portraits, he couldn't help wondering if he would end up looking like them. Each one was portly, bald, and had jowls like a depressed bloodhound. The Hollowhills Johnsons certainly weren't the most chipper-looking bunch. His father hadn't looked like that, but he had certainly been heading in the right direction. All those society lunches had played havoc with the man's waistline. His grandfather was a dead spit of a red-cheeked old buzzard in a powdered wig, so much so that the two of them could have been twins.

By the time he reached the dining room, the banging had stopped. In its place was the sound of a heavy brush scraping bits of shattered masonry into a metal dustpan and the sound of muttering. Peering around the door, Bill saw that his grandfather had taken a lump hammer to the hearth and had utterly decimated the slates revealing the chipped stone beneath.

"Morning, Grandfather, is everything all right?" Bill asked.

George didn't respond. He just carried on sweeping and grumbling, his eyes fixed on the rubble at his feet.

"Grandfather?" This time, Bill said it louder and caught the man's attention.

"Hmm?" George looked up with a faraway look in his eyes.

"Are you well, Grandfather?"

"What?" After a few seconds of apparent absence, George's eyes came into focus. "Yes, quite all right, quite all right, yes. How's the finger, my lad?"

Bill held it up and shrugged. "What are you doing?"

George had returned his attention to the brush. "Hmm?" he asked distractedly. Once all the shards were in the scuttle, he bent down and picked it up. "Just removing temptation...just removing temptation." His words were a barely audible whisper that sent shivers up Bill's spine.

Bill watched him walk past and out to the dustbin. Something was wrong with George's demeanour. His eyes were vacant and his movements slow, almost dreamlike. Bill shrugged as he pondered George's words. A bee in his bonnet, indeed. Once his brain caught up with what had transpired, he was upset, not because he particularly liked the tile work, but because he hadn't yet solved the mystery of the symbol. He could see the stark lines in vivid blood-red and charcoal-black every time he closed his eyes.

Stepping inside the dining room, carefully stepping around the sharp shards of masonry that George had missed, Bill started to look amongst the detritus for the page from his sketchbook. Disappointment welled up inside him as he realised that, as was to be expected, the bloodied item had been disposed of. Soon, the scent of frying bacon announced that breakfast was ready.

♅♈♉♒

George never came in for breakfast that morning, which seemed to send Iris into some kind of nervous state. She wrung her hands and battered her boiled egg with her spoon as though she had electric current fizzing up her backside. Bill didn't notice, however, he was too busy alternating between jamming a bacon sandwich between his gums and trying to recreate the symbol on his sketch pad. By the time he had finished eating, he had a passible facsimile to base his investigations upon.

Iris told Viola that George was prone to occasional "attacks of melancholy" to explain away his strange behaviour that morning, and proceeded to list all the different types of tea and herbal infusions that she administered to soothe his nerves. Bill, inevitably, found this talk of chamomile and lavender supremely tedious and excused himself. He was determined to find out more about the symbol from the hearth. Mysteries are irresistible to a child, especially when they are linked to pain and misery, and Bill went hurrying off to the library to get started on his investigation.

The Johnson family library was almost overwhelming in its scale. The generations of owners had accumulated books on everything from alchemy to zoology. Luckily, George kept a meticulous cataloguing system to aid in the location of what the reader desired. The categories were referenced by shelf and section making it a cinch to lay your hands on a volume about pruning rhododendrons, should the urge take you. Though, his family's love of flowers was something that must have skipped a generation when it came to Bill. The love of books, however… From a very young age, William Johnson was an accomplished and voracious reader.

Convinced that the symbol was somehow occult in nature, Bill opened the ledger and skipped to the relevant page. Due to the sheer amount of books in the room, he was somewhat perplexed to find a single historical work listed under both *occult* and *witchcraft*: Cotton Mather's *Wonders of the Physical World*. The rest were works of fiction. The only other thing on the *occult* page was a series of numbers scribbled in the bottom left corner: 22, 33, 55, 11. Bill assumed that these were just page numbers and quickly ignored them. Finding

Mather's book to be completely lacking in pictures and written in an archaic dialect that he simply couldn't fathom, he reluctantly deemed his investigation to be over before it had started.

For a few days following the accident, Bill found that his hearing had been somehow enhanced. Following that hellish buzzing, he found himself able to hear the slightest stirring of the house. Every creaking timber and rustling curtain came through loud and clear. It struck him as odd that other sounds, such as Viola's voice, hadn't been similarly amplified. It only lasted for a handful of days, but during that time, Bill became a nervous wreck as every scrabble of a mouse under the floorboards made him flinch alarmingly. Mercifully, it quickly faded and he forgot all about it.

Aside from this, the only other events of that time that struck Bill as in any way odd was his grandfather's reaction when he later learned that Dr. Lester had been inside the house. Bill could hear him in the room below ranting and raving as he lay in bed after supper one evening. He was absolutely livid with Iris that Lester had been allowed inside. Bill made a mental note to ask Iris about it come morning, but, alas, he forgot. That was yet another mystery that would have to wait until another day.

On the plus side of things, Viola had been entirely correct in her assumption that Bill's finger would be the talk of the tiny one-room school across the green. On his first day, it was still bandaged and the day he finally took them off was like the grand unveiling of some lost masterpiece. Boys gasped and girls swooned as they looked upon his scarred and truncated finger with a kind of repulsed awe. Nobody had anything close to his scar, not even the girl who got her finger stuck in a cuckoo clock could rival his injury. Though, that one did admittedly have more comedy value.

Still, it took Bill a good while to adjust to his new life in Hollowhills. Eventually, it became the only home he would ever truly have. Bill was destined to never leave.

~II~

The Tree and The Shadow

For the next couple of years, things in Hollowhills seemed to pass without major incident as Bill slowly but surely settled into his new life. Sure, there were the scrapes, cuts, and knocks that every child endures, but nothing that could be classed as *unusual*. George had become a solid influence in his life and, contrary to all expectations, had readily agreed to his choosing an academic life. Bill was never what you could call adept at physical activity and much preferred to spend his free time in the library devouring volume after volume. Recalling his late father's bile concerning George's insistence that he take up the miner's life, Bill was expecting a much different outcome.

"You have a real taste for books, don't you, lad?" George stated flatly over supper one evening.

"I like reading," Bill answered between mouthfuls of Susan's superb mutton broth. "I like to lose myself in books. Books are so much more interesting than life. I learn more from one of these old books than I do in a month at *that* school."

"That's probably right enough. Old Mistress Green is somewhat limited as a teacher, God bless the silly old crone." George smiled, then peered over his spectacles at his grandson, his bushy eyebrows bristling. "Well, perhaps we should think about getting you into the Truro School? You know, the posh new one they have just finished building? You could study there and then toddle off to university, become a proper little scholar." He got a faraway look in his eyes as he looked around the room slowly before muttering softly, "It would probably do you good to get out from under this roof."

This, Bill wasn't prepared for. A wide grin spread across his face as he nodded enthusiastically. "I would like that. To learn, I mean...not leave you, Grandfather."

George hummed thoughtfully as he jammed a hunk of crusty bread into his maw. "Very well. I'll see to it." His attention returned to his repast, signifying that the conversation was at an end.

That was it. That was the discussion. A life decision made as quickly as ordering a drink. They spent the rest of the meal in stoic silence, but Bill's heart was dancing with joy. The prospect of being forced into the mines after his schooling was complete had been looming over him like the Sword of Damocles. As he mopped up the last of the broth with a slice of bread, an unexpected feeling spread through him. Bill couldn't put his finger on it, but it seemed to stem from his realisation that the modern Truro School was a boarding school. Why this should have upset him was a complete mystery. Hadn't he wanted to return to Truro in the first place? After a moment, Bill waved it away as nerves. Nerves…and Kirsten.

Kirsten Gloyn, the girl with the cuckoo clock, had quickly become Bill's best friend in the whole world. She was a pretty girl his own age who, like Bill, had little interest in the things that captivated the rest of their peers. She too was blessed with a keen mind and a love of reading. They bonded over the works of Coleridge, "The Rime of the Ancient Mariner" was a personal favourite of hers. It resonated deeply as she viewed her family legacy, mine workers of high standing, to be her own personal albatross, a feeling that Bill could surely empathise with.

When told of his grandfather's plan to send him away to Truro, Kirsten was bursting with enthusiasm; they were both of the age that they were trying to figure out what to do with their lives. "You've got to go, Will," she enthused. She was the only person who called him Will. He didn't mind it from her; it was almost like a pet name. Their friendship was starting to blossom into something much more serious. "You *'ave* to, you know what will 'appen if you stay 'ere, you'll end up down the pit bent an' crooked like an old stick."

Bill shrugged. He was slightly put out by her enthusiasm. "I don't know. I won't see you for weeks on end."

"I'll still be 'ere when you get back. I'm not goin' anywhere. Ma has got me a live-in position at the Conley's. She can't wait to get shot of me."

"It sounds like you can't wait to get shot of *me*." Bill frowned and looked down at the grass as a shadow fell over them.

"Don't be ruddy silly!" Kirsten chuckled musically. "I just don't want you getting' sent down the pit. You're too clever by half for that sort of life."

Flattery, combined with the way she snuggled up to him on the damp grass of the large lawn made his fears crumble and his spirits sour, and after more conversation and reassurances, Bill set his mind to leave the village.

♎︎♓︎♒︎♑︎

True to his word, George had indeed set the wheels of change into motion. When Bill turned sixteen, he was informed that he would be packed off to the boarding school at the next term intake. Dizzy with the speed of it all, Bill couldn't help thinking that George wanted to get rid of him. Maybe he was a burden, a thorn in his porcine side? That same paranoid feeling he had experienced with Kirsten came back to the fore, and his mind raced towards the direst of conclusions. Not for a single second did he consider that his grandfather was doing it to save him.

Three days before his departure, Bill had risen, broken his fast, and shared a nice cup of tea on the patio with Viola. The poor woman was distraught; Bill had been so wrapped up in himself that he hadn't even considered that she was now soon to be out of a job. Cursing his selfishness, Bill assured her that George would find a position for her. Iris wasn't getting any younger, and could use the help. Viola brightened somewhat at this thought. After all, she had been more of a housekeeper than a governess for a couple of years by that point.

George seemed to like having the bright young woman around, possibly as a counterpoint to Iris' increasingly nervous nature. The two ladies balanced each other nicely, and it wasn't as though he didn't have room. Feeling slightly better about things, Viola returned to the house to aid Susan with something or other, leaving Bill sitting in the sun feeling slightly guilty about departing. It was like something was conspiring to keep him in Hollowhills. Telling himself it was all in his head, he decided to go for a wander around the village.

The nearest dwelling to his own was Conley House to the east. The master of the house was the eldest of two brothers and was a former teacher at the old Truro school. He briefly considered going and asking him some questions about what he should expect, but one look at his hatchet-faced housekeeper, Mrs. Gittings, quickly changed his mind. That particular harridan made Iris look like a veritable ray of sunshine. As Bill leaned on the gate, he could see that she was at that time engaged in giving their odd-job man, Jack, a thorough ear-bashing. The poor old chap looked like his brain was melting from the heat of her words.

Deciding that discretion was the better part of valour, Bill turned towards the village green and started walking in the direction of the church. As he neared the small pond outside the school, Bill was surprised to see Kirsten sitting in the reeds with a couple of classmates surrounded by a knot of bulbous green toads. They didn't see Bill as he made his approach and his heart nearly stopped as he witnessed her land a kiss on the elder boy Tom's cheek. All rational thought escaped his mind as a dark shadow fell across the green. A harsh and chill wind rushed up the legs of his shorts and planted icy kisses on his nether regions.

She couldn't even wait for you to leave.

A hollow voice echoed in Bill's head as rage spread from the tips of his toes to the white knuckles of his clenched fists. Fighting the urge to explode into acts of extreme violence, Bill marched back towards the house with the shadow hanging heavy over his head. Bill felt like he had been betrayed. Like Kirsten had jammed a large icicle into his heart. The cold at the base of his spine wanted vengeance. It wanted to bash Tom's brains in with a log, then drown his brother and his duplicitous girlfriend in the festering pond.

Let the toads and newts use their lifeless bodies as homes for their spawn and let the maggots multiply and the fungi bloom. Death and glorious corruption is all that they deserve.

Bill's vision narrowed to a hazy throbbing tunnel of shadow as the awful buzzing returned to his ears. It started as a whisper then built to a scream as his body shook in fury. The bright sunshine became a flame, searing his freckled skin as beads of sticky sweat cascaded off his forehead. Only the shadow that loomed overhead stopped him from self-combusting. It protected him like a cocoon, sealing him away from the world, keeping him alone with his rage. Bill desperately needed to take his anger out on something—something that didn't fight back.

Storming through the house, ignoring Susan's cheery greeting, Bill left via the double doors in the library and marched out into the garden. George Johnson owned two acres of garden divided into several sections. There was the main lawn, a vegetable garden, herb garden, rockery, pond, and what he called the top or secret garden. This was shielded on all sides by densely packed trees and shrubs. It was raised about six feet above the rest of the garden, and was accessed by seven cracked and moss-stained steps running under a tangled rose arch that had been invaded by ivy and brambles. It was totally hidden from the house and the rest of the village; no prying eyes could see what went on in that secretive place, and it was to that sanctuary that he fled.

Following the serpentine path through the herb garden, Bill tried to concentrate on steadying his breathing; he was panting like a dog in heat. Every breath felt like razor cuts and sent his pulse racing faster and faster. He was in the grip of such intense anger that it bordered on a seizure. His muscles were tense, his skin taut, his joints cracked, and his teeth ground together, sending pain through his jaw and up to his temples. All the while, his brain echoed with hateful words:

You can't leave here…she will forget you. Everyone will forget you. You belong here. You mustn't leave. You can't leave… Punish them… Punish them all.

Over and over the words raced like a speeding carousel with twisted horses wearing the laughing faces of Kirsten and the two Green boys. Round and round, faster and faster, with the buzzing in his ears swirling and sweeping like a cyclone. Bill wanted to scream for it to stop, just drop to his knees in pain and overwhelming mental anguish. Anything to make it stop. He wanted to bury his head in the soil, but something kept him going, kept pushing him onwards into deeper pits of incandescent fury.

Rustling through the overgrown arch, pitching forwards at such an acute angle that it was a miracle that he didn't land flat on his face, Bill headed for the sheds at speed. George had constructed two large sheds side-by-side on the left-hand side of the top garden. One was a basic affair used for tool storage, the other was his own personal sanctuary, complete with a deck chair and a reading desk. Behind these weathered structures he had erected a lean-to using old windows and timbers from a previous renovation. Opening the storage shed, Bill paused for a second before selecting a sturdy axe handle and testing it against his palm—it was perfect.

Skirting the fire circle in the centre of the garden, growling and snarling through his firmly clenched teeth, Bill made his way towards the line of conifers that lined the rear fence. He didn't know why he chose those particular trees for a sound thrashing, but that is indeed what they received. As he reared back and brought the sturdy wooden bludgeon in a swinging arc, again and again, Bill howled like one of the hounds of the underworld. The heavy *thunk* of wood against wood was the only sound that could penetrate the awful buzzing in his ears. Every impact was accompanied by the sneering and laughing faces of Kirsten and the Green brothers.

Bill thrashed away at the increasingly damaged trees with every ounce of strength he possessed until the whispering voices subsided and he collapsed to the ground, completely spent. Gradually, his blinkered vision widened and his breathing became steady as he rolled onto his back and peered up through the canopy of the surrounding trees. The shadow above him dissipated and shrank into the tree-line taking the vestiges of his fury with it. His eyes were stinging from the tears that now flooded down his cheeks in thick torrents. Hugging the axe handle to his chest, Bill lay there for what seemed like hours, quietly sobbing to himself.

Eventually, whatever had inflicted him subsided, and he managed to get a grip on his emotions. The rustle of the strong breeze through the foliage became a soothing melody as he sat and pondered over what had just transpired. Bill hadn't felt like himself at all; it was almost as though something had invaded his head and driven his hand. The rear of the garden was now a mess of fallen needles, strips of bark, and split branches. A moment of fear at what his grandfather would say hit him, but he quickly buried it by reasoning that it was all George's fault for trying to get rid of him. The silly old fool should be glad that it was only a few ratty trees that got a good hiding. Bill had momentarily forgotten that it was *his* desire to leave that had sparked his relative into action in the first place.

Returning the axe handle to the shed and bolting the door, Bill suddenly felt refreshed, as though an oppressive weight had been lifted from his chest. *He* didn't have to leave if *he* didn't want to. If Bill wanted to stay in Hollowhills, then he jolly well would! Chuckling to himself, he decided to enjoy the remainder of the afternoon. Having no desire to see anyone, especially Kirsten, he chose to stay in his secluded spot and enjoy the fine weather.

The fire pit was surrounded by four large trees, two apple, an ash, and a twisted sycamore. Over the years, the sycamore had become *his* tree; it was perfect for climbing and had two junctions between limbs that were ideal for sitting and peering out onto the sweeping hills of Bodmin moor. In the distance, he could see his grandfather's mine. The people looked tiny and insignificant as they swarmed the muddy ground, pushing carts and lifting shovels.

"Maybe becoming a miner wouldn't be too bad..." he mused aloud as he climbed up to the highest perch.

Bill sat and inhaled the salt breeze that drifted in from the coast as he gazed out at the rocky outcrop known locally as 'The Edge.' Even that far inland, there was a distinct tang of rotten seaweed; it may sound revolting, but combined with the sweetness of the early spring blossom, it was something of a tonic. Bill stripped leaves off a spindly twig and thought again about leaving. Suddenly, his previous epiphany seemed utterly ridiculous. He wanted to leave. The last thing he wanted was to be stuck in that nowhere place for the remainder of his life. Where those contrary thoughts came from was a complete mystery. After a few minutes of calm reflection, he was starting to feel like his old self again.

One of Bill's favourite subjects to read about was biology. Not the trite birds and bees stuff that was spoon-fed in the schoolhouse, but real biology. As a subscriber to Darwin's Theory of Evolution, a fact that upset the deeply religious Iris, he occasionally liked to indulge his primitive side by having a good old swing from the branches. Above his favoured seat was an overhanging branch that was the perfect size and strength for swinging on, and he had spent many a happy hour kicking his legs in the air and whooping like a monkey. Standing upright, he edged over to the branch, gripped it firmly, and swung out.

Swinging back and forth, Bill focused directly ahead. The ground rushed in a smear of brown, green, and the blinding blue of the heavens. It was so hypnotic that he could have swung for hours if his puny arms would have allowed. The weightlessness of his feet and the pull of gravity on his joints was an awesome sensation that he missed when his feet were firmly planted on *terra firma*. After a couple of minutes of dangling, his palms began to chafe, and his fingers grew tired and weak.

Almost at the point of stopping and lowering himself to the ground, Bill spotted something move in his peripheral vision. He only caught a glimpse of it for a fraction of a second as his legs kicked skyward. A chill exploded in his guts as he craned his neck to get a better look. There was definitely something there, just in the tree line of the boundary. Bill swung again, this time looking directly in the shadow's direction. Bill let out a horrified yelp. It seemed to be slightly closer. Another swing, and it was closer still. He was too terrified to stop swinging, as though it wasn't actually there if he saw it through blurred vision. It was vaguely humanoid in shape, but somehow fragmented, like a man-shaped swarm of blowflies or midges.

Shutting his eyes, Bill told himself over and over that there was nothing there, that it was just a trick of the light. When he opened them, it was standing under the nearest tree, out of the boundary and in the garden itself. Something appeared to be creeping up on him, stalking him, waiting until it was out of his line of sight before taking swift footsteps towards him.

The ferocious buzzing returned to his ears once again, but at a higher pitch than ever before. Bill couldn't do anything but just keep swinging, until…

Crack!

Bill bellowed in surprise as the branch suddenly gave way. It came cleanly away from the limb when he was at the apex of the swing with his feet pointing towards the figure. Something gripped his ankles and pulled. Gravity is a vicious beast when it strikes without warning. Bill plummeted to earth still clutching the branch in both hands. All the wind was driven out of his body as he landed pancake flat on his back on the firm ground. The rear of his head connected with an exposed tree root and the severed branch slammed into his face. A hollow cackle drifted on the breeze as pain took hold of his senses, and everything went black.

Bill found himself sitting in the rocking chair at his parents' home in Truro. The fire in the hearth roared and crackled and rain pitter-pattered on the plate glass windows. Looking around the dimly-lit room, his eyes darted from memory to memory. It was his home the night before his parents went to sea. The night before they drowned. It was cosy and serene, the only sound besides the crackle of wood was the heavy *tick-tock* of the grandfather clock and the gentle breathing of his mother.

"Mummy?" he whispered, barely audible.

His mother, Bettany, looked up from her book and smiled. Her features were slightly smudged, blurred by the years without her. Her blonde hair, always immaculate, rustled almost imperceptibly as a shadow moved on the wall behind her.

Focusing on the walls, Bill waved it away as the effect of the flames. "I miss you, Mummy."

Bettany's eyes twinkled. There was something in her gaze that he didn't remember, her eyes were cold. "I know, dear." The corners of her mouth twitched as a mocking smile spread across her face. "But I don't miss you."

His mother's words were like a kick to the guts. "Mummy? What do you mean?"

"What do you think I mean, stupid child!"

Bill yelped in surprise as she bolted forward in her chair, hurling the heavy old tome at his head. It clattered off the back of his chair and tumbled to the floor. Looking down, the cover snapped open, and the pages flipped forward and back at an alarming rate. The noise of the fluttering paper rose to a deafening pitch, to that dreadful buzzing noise that threatened to rupture his eardrums. Transfixed by the book, he didn't see the shadow of the hand that fell onto his shoulder.

"She means, you idiot, that we didn't want you. We never wanted you."

"Father?" Looking up into his father Steven's face, tears flowed from his eyes in torrents.

"Why do you think we always went away?" Bettany added. Turning to her, Bill's sobs turned to screams as half of his mother's face bled, cracked, and crumbled away, leaving the disturbing visage he had seen once before in his nightmares.

Steven's bones cracked and creaked as he shuffled in front of the fire. He too looked like a walking corpse. "We should have left you on the steps of the church. That would have saved us all the trouble, wouldn't it have, my love?"

Bettany giggled musically, but there was another sound underneath it, a warping of the notes that gave it a daemonic cadence. "Oh, it certainly would."

Shadows from the corners of the room started to vibrate and spread up the walls like a liquid, gathering along with the intensity of the buzzing. Bill's blood was boiling in his veins; anger at their words was driving him into a violent rage.

Rising to join her husband at the fireplace, Bettany giggled girlishly. "Maybe we should have tossed him into the river? Let the fish have him."

Their twisted and mangled bodies had eclipsed the glow of the fire. The only thing that remained was shadow.

This was all that Bill could stand. He jumped to his feet and grabbed the poker from next to the hearth. "I hate you!" he bellowed as he raised his arm and prepared to strike.

That's it, Will, Willy, William… Bash their brains in, Bill, Billy, Boy…

"Stop it, please!" he screamed at the unknown voice that plagued him. Clamping his hands to his ears, he let the poker clatter to the floor. "Just…leave me alone!"

As the corpses of his parents leered and mocked his struggle, a warm hand touched his shoulder and turned him around. Bill nearly choked on his tears as he saw his mother and father standing there looking warm and healthy.

"You let it taste you, William. It knows you. It wants to wear you," Bettany said with sorrow.

"You need to leave here," Steven added. "Get far away from here, before it is too late."

Taking his parents' hands, he walked towards the door. The twisted copies of his parents bellowed and screeched in fury. The shadow started to bubble and hiss on the walls, melting the wallpaper and turning the plaster to dust.

Kill them, Bill, Billy, Will, Willy… Kill them all… Let me inside…

Rippling coils of shadow burst from the walls and snapped around the necks of Bill's parents, squeezing and constricting their heads. Bill backed away and covered his eyes as the voice in his head cackled maniacally and the tentacles tightened.

Splat!

♀♻♉♓

"No!"

Bill's eyes snapped open, staring up at the fat globs of icy rain that fell from the glowering clouds above the top garden. The sickening sound of his parents' heads popping rang in his ears. His clothes stuck to his saturated skin as he groaned and tried to focus. How long he'd been out was a mystery, but it was long enough for a storm to have rolled in off the sea.

Sitting up slowly, pain radiated from his mouth and the back of his head pounded. The world lurched like it had just wobbled on its axis. Rolling onto his side, Bill grabbed the grass for dear life as everything spun and blurred around him.

With the back of his hand, he wiped his mouth and was horrified to see that it came away covered in dark clots of blood. Using a questing finger, he felt along his lip and discovered an inch-long gash. Blood had also pooled and crusted on his upper lip from his nose.

The branch had both lacerated him and broken his nose. Bill was a mess.

Despite the pouring rain, he didn't feel cold. On the contrary, his body still burned with the rage from his dream. His mind was in turmoil; he both loved and hated his parents. No matter how he looked at it, he still saw them as abandoning him. He could count the amount of quality time he'd spent with them both on the fingers of his left leg. No, it had been Viola and Viola alone that had cared for him. How could he leave her? He couldn't... He *wouldn't*.

The wind rustling in the branches of the sycamore tree sounded like the chuckling of a distant presence. Bill snapped his head around in fear as the shadow figure that had caused his tumble flashed back into his memory. Peering into the corners of the garden, his vision seemed to take a fraction of a second to catch up with his eyeballs. His movements were sluggish as he tried to push himself up onto his knees. The knock to his head had dulled his motor functions and sent his nervous system haywire.

Bile rose in the back of his throat as he stood, and using the tree for support, he purged onto the exposed roots. The pressure in his head was immense, his eyeballs felt heavy and bloated. Feeling the back of his head, he was shocked to find another laceration and a lump the size of a duck egg. Thick clots had adhered his hair to his scalp, brushing one with his truncated finger tore away a clump of hairs. Wincing afresh, he leaned back and tried to stand fully upright.

Crack! Crack! Crack!

Spinning in the direction of the conifers nearly sent him sprawling back to the ground. Holding onto the trunk, he watched in confusion as the bewilderingly intact trees were thrashed by unseen hands. He was watching his rage-fueled handiwork take place before his eyes. His mouth, dripping with saliva, twisted into a satisfied smirk.

If they had only been people…

As soon as those hateful words crossed his mind, Bill cried out in horror; these thoughts, these dreadful urges, they couldn't possibly be his own—could they? Screwing his eyes tightly shut, he tried to clear his mind and get some kind of a grip on reality. With great effort, he managed to push the rage aside and retrieve his rational mind from the clutches of the Stygian shadow that had begun to make a home in his frontal lobe. Opening his eyes, he was glad to see that the trees were back to how he had left them after his tantrum. The spectral sounds of his attack and the buzzing had subsided and were being swallowed by the cacophonous din of shaking leaves, creaking tree limbs, and the relentless hiss of the rain.

"Come on, Bill. Get a hold of yourself. You've had a bit of a knock on the head, that's all."

The pain that had been lurking at the back of his mind suddenly came hurtling to the fore. Grabbing the back of his head, he grimaced as sharp stabs of trauma shot down his neck. Once it had subsided, he became fully aware of his situation. It was as though the pain had helped him lift the shadow somehow. Like it had cleansed his mind in some way. Embracing the reality of pain, he let go of the sycamore tree and stumbled in the direction of the overgrown rose arch.

A flash of lightning lit the trees as Bill tried to get his legs to do as they were told. His joints were rubbery and every step felt like the ground was spongy. Passing the ash tree, he suddenly stopped. He had just caught sight of something in the corner of his eye. Something was lurking in the corner of the garden. Bill didn't want to look, he had endured just as much as he was capable of enduring. Slowly, hesitantly, he turned his head. There was nothing there.

"Stop it. You're just seeing things. Just…*breathe*." He tried to focus on the words Viola used to say when he had suffered a nightmare. Smiling weakly at the thought, he resumed walking.

By now, the wind had risen to such force that the rose arch had become a hazard of flailing strands of spiky bramble and whip-like fronds of ivy. Hugging his arms to his body, he ducked under the wild vegetation and mounted the steps.

You can't leave!

Bill found himself airborne as he was shoved forcefully off the steps. The angry words were accompanied by a roar of thunder and a *crackle* of electricity. Trying to roll through the landing, Bill pitched forward, scraping his knees raw on the stone path. Using the momentum, he regained his footing and careened into a privet hedge, scratching his arms and face.

Crying with the pain and shaking uncontrollably, he turned and saw what had pushed him. It was Steven. His father's face was contorted into a cruel rictus as he took the steps with jerky, shuddering movements. He was clutching the axe handle in one hand and playfully slapping it against the other.

"Whack-whack, William… Whack-whack!"

Bill broke into a run. Well, as close to a run as he could manage under the circumstances. Steven's words sounded strange. The tone was all wrong; it sounded somehow mangled like he was gargling custard or had a mouthful of jellied eels. Then, there were the man's eyes. Gone was the steely-grey, replaced by two bruised pits of inky shadow.

Tumbling headlong through the herb garden, snagging his clothing on the flailing rosemary and lavender bushes, Bill raced away from the horrific revenant of his dead father. Reaching the main lawn, his legs buckling under him and his feet slipping on the slick grass, he focused on the house and tried to keep going. The buzzing had returned and the back of his head throbbed. With each pound, the shadows at the edges of his vision deepened and crept further in. Soon, his vision was nothing more than a narrow tunnel with a blurred smudge at the end.

Stumbling down the steps to the yard, his knees finally gave up the fight, and he plunged to his hands and knees, wheezing and choking. Blood was pouring from his lacerated lip and pooling onto the stone before mingling with the rainwater. As he shook and convulsed, waiting for his father to bring the bludgeon down on his head and put him out of his misery, Susan emerged from the kitchen and wailed in alarm.

"My God in Heaven! Master Bill...whatever 'as 'appened?!" She swept across the yard, splashing dirty water all over her apron. Wrapping him in her arms, she raised his head and gasped. His eyes had rolled back in his head, showing only white orbs threaded with angry red veins. "Iris...! Viola...! Some-bugger, help!"

Wiping his mouth with a bundled up handful of her dripping wet apron, Susan tried to bring Bill round. "Can you 'ear me? What 'appened?"

Bill's jaw moved up and down, but no intelligible words came out. What tumbled from his larynx was a guttural discharge of syllables, clicks, and grunts. "Hup n'ghftnahh h' nog ahfhtagnor!"

"What's the matter, Susan?" Iris crowed as her head appeared around the door.

"It's young Bill, Iris. He looks like he's been in the wars and no mistake. The poor bugger is covered in blood, look!"

"Good heavens," Iris gasped as she trotted primly over to them.

"I think he's hit 'is head. There's one heck of a lump back here."

"Hup n'ghftnahh h' nog ahfhtagnor!" Bill gasped, his teeth rattling furiously.

"Hush. Don't try to speak, luv," Susan cooed, stroking his forehead. "Help me get 'im inside. 'E's chilled to the bone, the poor mite."

Taking his legs, Iris helped Susan bundle him towards the door. Susan was used to humping sacks of spuds around, so a stick-thin schoolboy was no trouble, and Iris was much tougher than she looked.

"Any idea what happened?" Iris grunted as she backed up the doorstep.

"No idea. I was taking some tater peelin's out to compost when 'e came crashin' into the yard like 'e'd been shot out of a ruddy cannon. Gave me a right scare, it did."

"We need to get him warm; he'll catch his death at this rate."

"Over by the oven, I'm renderin' down some pig fat. It should be nice and toasty." Susan grabbed a bundle of dishcloths off the table, rolled them up, and placed them under Bill's head as they laid him down by the oven door.

"Right, check his wounds while I fetch some blankets," Iris instructed. "I'll send Viola for the doctor."

A sharp intake of breath from Susan made Iris scowl. "Are ye sure that's wise, Iris? George was fair incandescent after the last time."

Pursing her lips and strengthening her resolve, Iris started for the stairs. "I don't care. *He*'s not here, and *his* grandson is terribly injured. This blasted feud has gone on for far too long. He needs a doctor, and that's that!"

Watching her leave, Susan muttered under her breath, "On your head be it."

♕♛♖♟

Viola was engaged in scrubbing the master bedroom floor with a hand brush and a bucket of carbolic when Iris swept into the room. "Viola, there you are. Go and fetch Dr. Lester, immediately."

"What?"

"Don't just sit there gawping like a beached haddock, woman. Fetch the doctor, now!"

"But…what about Master George?" Viola stood and flattened down her rumpled pinny.

"There's no time for that nonsense. Bill is injured…severely. Tell the doctor to come right away." Iris's shoes clip-clopped on the floorboards as she pirouetted out of the room in the direction of the linen closet.

Viola didn't want to go against the master's wishes, but she would rather tangle with him than an irate Iris.

She was terrifying when her blood was up. George was all bluster while Iris was vicious. Viola had once witnessed her reduce the local baker's boy to tears with just a few lashes of her razor-sharp tongue. Formidable was an understatement.

Trotting out of the room and down to the ground floor, she could hear Bill babbling incoherently and had to fight the urge to go to him. Susan was with him and she would have trusted the benevolent cook with her life, but still, she felt a pang of guilt for not being at his side. The almost-fraternal bond that Bill felt for Viola went both ways.

Hurriedly retrieving a battered umbrella from the hat stand next to the door, she exited the house and stepped into the fierce rain. It was coming down in icy rods by now, and the umbrella did little to protect her. She was soaked to the skin by the time she reached the gate. Despite it being only mid-afternoon, the thick black storm clouds had gathered in such density that one could have mistaken it for nightfall.

Normally, she would have taken the road that wound around the village green, especially in inclement weather, but the urgency in Iris' voice made her break with tradition and race onto the grass. Realising her mistake almost instantly, Viola soon found herself up to her ankles in mud and fighting to keep her balance. As she neared the midpoint of the green, a mighty gust of wind caught her umbrella and yanked it from her grasp. Cursing in a decidedly unladylike manner, she watched it sail away and land in the pond with a *splosh*.

"Hell's teeth. George will have my guts for garters if I don't get that back." Biting her lip, she unsteadily followed the parasol in an attempt to retrieve it. If it had been her own, she would have left it, but it belonged to George and he didn't take kindly to people using his things at the best of times, let alone abandoning them in the pond.

Carefully approaching the bank, Viola gave a little yelp of alarm when she found herself being eyed with suspicion by hundreds of croaking toads. Their cold gaze was unnerving in the extreme. On the verge of giving up the umbrella for lost, she was startled to find two naked boys splashing around in the reeds, seemingly playing with the amphibians. It was Tom and Jeremy Green.

Dumbfounded, Viola gave a discreet cough before addressing them. "*Ahem*, could you possibly pass me my umbrella?"

Jeremy Green stopped his splashing and eyed her with the same dead-eyed look as the assembled batrachian horde. Tom, however, grinned warmly. "Oh, hello, Miss Viola. I was wondering where that came from. Lovely day for a swim, isn't it?"

"Um…" Viola didn't know how to respond to that. "What are you two boys playing at? You'll catch your death!"

"Nah," Tom chuckled as he waded over to the umbrella. "Me and my brother 'ere like a good splash in the pond. Especially during a storm. It's actually quite warm. Ye should try it sometime, miss."

She shook her head emphatically. "No, I don't think so, Tom."

"Suit yerself. Here you go, miss." He handed the umbrella over and dived under the water, wriggling away like a tadpole.

Throughout the exchange, Jeremy hadn't moved a muscle. He hadn't even blinked.

"Thank you, boys." Viola nodded graciously as she forced the twisted device shut and tucked it under her arm.

Again, Jeremy remained impassive.

With a chill coursing through her bones, she turned away and hastened in the direction of Dr. Lester's home-cum-surgery. It was strange, but she could feel

Jeremy's eyes on her back, watching her approach Lester's door—Jeremy *and* his croaking friends.

Knock! Knock! Knock!

"Come on, Doctor." Viola blew on her hands and stamped her feet on the flagstone path to ward off the cold.

Knock! Knock! Knock!

Viola pressed her ear to the door. She could hear ponderous footsteps moving with an infuriating lack of urgency. "Doctor...? Doctor Lester?"

Lester didn't reply.

KNOCK-KNOCK-KNOCK!

Finally, the door opened. Dr. Lester peered down at Viola and smiled. "My dear Viola, what brings you out on a day like this?"

"Oh, Dr. Lester. It's Bill, he's frightfully injured."

"Oh, dear. I'm afraid that I can't help you. George made it perfectly clear the last time—"

Viola cut him off. "But, he needs a doctor, urgently. Iris says that he's in an awful state."

Lester pinched the bridge of his nose. "But—"

Again, Viola cut him short. "Must I remind you of the Hippocratic oath, *Doctor*?"

With a sigh of resignation, Lester surrendered. "Very well. Let me get my coat. But, only if George isn't around. He hates me with a passion that borders on the monomaniacal."

While the doctor put on his hat and Inverness cape, and picked up his Gladstone bag, Viola decided to try to get some answers. "Why is that, Doctor? What happened between you two?"

Lester smiled innocently. "I'm sure I don't know. He and my father used to be friends, but they had a parting of the ways. I have done nothing wrong."

Viola wasn't convinced. She had no real reason to distrust Lester, but a certain *something* was lurking beneath his avuncular facade that made her skin crawl. Still waters run deep, and all that. She was sure that Lester wasn't entirely what he seemed. "Have you tried reasoning with the man?"

"What would be the point?" Lester stepped outside, shut and locked the door. "He's a bull-headed man, as I'm sure you well know by now. Once he has taken against you, that's it. There is no reasoning with the man. Just ask his workers in the tin mine."

Leading the way back across the green, Viola's interest was piqued by this remark. "Oh? Whatever do you mean?"

Lester didn't reply. It was only now that she noticed that he had stopped dead in his tracks and was looking over at the pond with an odd look on his face.

"Doctor?"

No response. Lester was as still as a headstone.

"Dr. Lester?"

"Um…what?" He turned to look at her. "Sorry, I was miles away for a moment there Toads."

"Pardon?"

"Toads, my dear. I'm afraid that I have a fear of the beasts. Bufonophobia, I believe it's called. I read an interesting paper on the subject of phobias in—"

"Doctor! Can we get on? I can't feel my fingers." Viola was rapidly losing patience with Lester's dithering.

"Quite right. Forgive me. Take me to the young Master Bill." Pulling his cape around his chest, he hurried after Viola, trying to focus his mind on the task at hand.

♕ʓʓ♍

"Father, no!"

"Hush, now. You've 'ad a nasty knock on the 'ead." Susan dabbed gently at Bill's face with a damp flannel, removing the crusty blood from his nose and mouth.

Bill's eyes finally rolled back around as his babbling ceased and he became aware of his surroundings. "What…? Wha…Susan? What's going on?"

"Stay still, ye've done yourself a proper mischief. Try not to talk. Your lip's gonna need some stitches."

"Where did he go?" Bill's eyes suddenly became wide with fear.

"Who? Did someone do this to you, Bill?"

"My father, he had a stick. 'Whack, Whack,' he said… Called me William. My name is Bill now… Damn the tree. The tree and the shadow… They did this… They want my flesh." Bill's eyelids fluttered, then closed as he finally lapsed into unconsciousness.

"Where is that girl? I bet that wretched doctor is being difficult." Iris paced the chequered kitchen tiles like a caged animal, wringing her hands and quietly stewing. "I'll give him a piece of my mind if he doesn't get here soon."

"Go easy on 'im, Iris." Susan sighed as she tucked the coarse blanket under Bill's chin. "Understandably, he'd be a touch apprehensive, what with George threatening him last time."

Iris scowled. "Pah! I should knock their ruddy heads together. Pig-headed men. I ask you, why do we put up with them?"

This made Susan smile. Iris' disdain for the male sex always did. Iris would have made a fine early advocate for women's liberation. "There are much worse masters than George, Iris. What about that lunatic across the way, Conley?"

Iris smirked at this. "That's true. Old Gittings must have the patience of a saint!"

"More of a devil, if ye ask me," Susan muttered almost inaudibly.

"Pardon?" Iris bristled. She and Gittings were old friends.

To Susan's relief, at that precise moment, the door slammed, and Viola scurried into the room looking like a drowned rat, followed by a furtive-looking Dr. Lester.

"There you are, Doctor," Iris greeted Lester primly. "About ruddy time."

Passing his sopping wet hat and coat to the equally saturated Viola, Lester harrumphed and waved Susan and Iris out of the way. "What happened?"

"We're not sure," Susan explained. "He came from the top garden with a bang on 'is 'ead and blood all over 'im. He was muttering something about a tree. I reckon he's 'ad a fall. He's always up that old sycamore, a proper little monkey, 'e is."

"Viola, pass me my bag, would you?"

Viola went to move, but Iris held her hand up and snapped at Lester, "I'll help you, Doctor. That poor thing needs to get out of those sopping clothes before she catches a chill." She turned to Viola with a smile. "Run along and change, dear."

"Thanks, Iris. I'll be back down in a few minutes."

"No, we'll be fine down here. Go and make up a nice warm bed for him. I have a feeling he's going to need it."

"Yes, Iris, right away," Viola said, leaving the room.

"Mmm," Lester hummed thoughtfully. "He's had a fall, all right. There is tree bark in his lip and soil in the head wound. I'll need to rinse them out before I can stitch them up. Did he say anything else before he passed out?"

"He was out of it, I'm afraid," Susan replied. "He was speaking in tongues and raving about his dead father…and a shadow."

"Shadow?" Lester's eyes took on sharpness as he snapped his head around to look at Susan.

"Yeah, the tree an' the shadow, that's what he said."

"The tree and *the shadow*…" Lester trailed off for a second or two before returning his gaze to Bill's injuries. "I think it'll be best if we get him into bed. Can you help me carry him, Susan?"

"Aye, Doctor." Susan smiled.

"I take it that you will need towels and hot water?" Iris asked as the others started to carry Bill out of the room.

"Indeed," Lester puffed in reply.

Iris turned and placed the heavy copper kettle on the stove. "A 'thank you' would've been nice. That blasted Doctor needs to learn some manners."

༶༶༶

Bill awoke to the sounds of raised voices down in the drawing-room below his room. His head was pounding and his vision fuzzy. Straining to hear what was going on, he tried to sit up but his body wouldn't work. His extremities felt like lead. A familiar feeling from his previous serious injury. It appeared that Dr. Lester had given him another dose of his *special* medicine.

The voices rose in volume and ferocity. It was his grandfather and Iris. They were now screaming at each other. Finally managing to shift in his bed slightly, he dislodged a book from his bedside table. It fell to the floor with a dull *thud*.

"What in Heaven?" Viola sprung forward in her chair, startling the life out of Bill. "Oh, Bill, you're awake. I must have nodded off."

"Where…? What happened?" Bill slurred, the swelling from the wound on his lip making it difficult to speak.

"Shh, dear. You've had a bit of a nasty accident. We think you fell out of a tree."

Bill creased his face in concentration. His thoughts and memories were scattered like pieces of a particularly complex jigsaw puzzle. "A tree…yes. I was swinging. The branch…it broke. I hit my head." Raising his arm sluggishly, he tried to feel the lump at the back of his head.

Viola took his hand gently and returned it to his side. "You mustn't mess with it. Dr. Lester has had to stitch you up."

"Lester? In here?" Suddenly, the din from below made sense. "Grandfather sounds angry."

Viola snorted derisively. "Angry doesn't cover it. He's furious that he was in the house again. That, and the state of his conifers." She glared pointedly at Bill.

"Oh. I remember. Sorry."

"It's not me you need to apologise to. Poor Iris is getting a mouthful, and no mistake."

"I can hear…" Bill sighed guiltily.

"What were you doing up there, hmm?" Viola rarely used her *governess voice*, so when she did, it had the cutting effect of a well-maintained rapier. "Attacking the trees like some kind of caveman."

"I was angry… I'd seen…"

"Angry? Well, next time you are *angry,* take it out on something other than your grandfather's conifers. Your grandmother planted them, you know?"

Bill was aghast, the guilt gnawing at his stomach. "I didn't… I'm very sorry."

Viola's anger dissipated at his contrition. "Oh, well, I'm sure there is no lasting damage done. Whatever were you so angry about, anyway?"

"Um, it's nothing. I-I don't want to talk about it."

"William?" Viola fixed him with a look that broke his resolve in an instant. Since he had started going by Bill, his given name had become reserved for rollickings and reprimands.

"Fine, I saw Kirsten. She was kissing Tom Green."

Viola looked at him with concern and slight annoyance. "If you don't want to tell me, that's fine. But please don't lie to me." Standing up, she crossed to the door and pulled it open.

"It's the truth!" Bill snapped back in reply. "She was over by the pond."

"Bill, I'm putting this down to the bang on your head, but you couldn't have seen Kirsten today. She went with her family to visit an ailing relative in Penzance early this morning. They won't be back for days."

Bill didn't hear what Viola said after that. His mind was spinning. Watching her leave, he placed his head back on the pillow and stared at the ominous shadows cast by the Davy lamp on the dresser. Something was wrong with him, of this, he was sure. Closing his eyes, he surrendered to the morphine once again and let oblivion take him.

☒☷☵☊

The following morning, Bill awoke to the smell of bacon and a feeling of dread. The atmosphere in the house was tense and had an almost tangible presence. Sun was streaming through a crack in the curtains, landing squarely across his eyes. His arm had a split-second delay between thinking that he wanted to move it and the limb actually moving, but he managed to shield his vision from the glare.

Rolling onto his side, then sweeping his feet to the floor and sitting upright, Bill felt a strange disconnection with his body. His nerves were firing at random, sending jolts down the backs of his legs.

Lester had mentioned to Viola when he left that Bill might have suffered a concussion; he didn't know this at the time, so his body acting oddly made him start to panic. The room spun and lurched as he stood upright. As his legs buckled, he fell to his hands and knees. Nausea rose from his belly and hurtled towards his gullet. Clamping his mouth shut, he spun on the floor and grabbed the chamber pot from under the bed just in time.

Once purged, Bill climbed to his feet using the bed for support. His mouth burned with the awful tastes of stomach acid, metallic adrenaline, and bitter morphine. He wanted to just curl up in a ball but he needed water. The jug that Viola had placed on the bedside table had become overturned during the night. The water had run through the cracks in the floorboards. Throwing a dressing gown over his striped pyjamas, Bill set out on an expedition to the kitchen.

As soon as he wobbled onto the landing, it became abundantly clear that there was trouble in paradise. Susan banged her pots and pans with a fury that he hadn't hitherto experienced. Their metallic *clang* and *clatter* echoed throughout the hall. Each step towards the staircase was a battle; it felt as though he was wading through treacle. The dizziness from the residual opiates in his system added to the fact that he had double-vision from the concussion made focusing on his intended direction a Herculean task.

Using the polished oak bannister as a guide as well as for support, Bill started his descent. The ancestral pictures leered down at him with malevolent glee. It was like they were taking pleasure in his disorientation. As he reached the bottom of the stairs, he thought for one awful second that the austere members of his family tree were laughing at him. It was only when he reached the library that he realised that it was sobbing. Peering through the crack in the open door, he saw to his surprise his grandfather with his head in his hands and his shoulders shaking uncontrollably.

"It's not polite to eavesdrop!" Bill nearly had a heart attack as Viola appeared behind him wearing a stern expression. "What are you doing out of bed, young man?"

"I…I need water. Just been sick."

Viola softened. "You poor thing. Come along to the kitchen, I'll get you a fresh jug from the well."

Bill nodded slowly, his eyes dilated and swimming in their sockets. "What's wrong with Grandfather?"

"I have no idea, and it's not polite to ask. Come along." Taking him by the hand, she steered his body towards the kitchen.

The sound of sizzling rashers was joined by a low muttering as Susan stomped around the kitchen table, seemingly in some kind of distress.

"Morning, Susan." Viola noted her expression. "Whatever's the matter?"

"Oh, Viola!" Susan's voice rose to a pitch that could rupture eardrums. "Terrible news, Iris has gone!"

"Gone? What do you mean, gone?"

"What do you think I mean? She's gone, left, done a runner, had it away on her toes. George gave her her marching orders."

"He fired her?" Viola's mouth gaped in shock.

"Aye, He sent her packing at first light. She were gone by the time I arrived!"

"Whatever for? Surely not because of the Dr. Lester business?"

"I'm not sure, but I imagine so, yes. Them two were goin' at it like hammer and chisel when I left last night. Ye should 'ave heard some of the language they were using…I nearly dropped the bucket of slops I was takin' for the pigs." The family next to her home were pig farmers and their prize porkers gorged themselves on scraps from all the local houses. It was something of a local tradition to ditch your slops at the Angove pig farm.

"I-I don't understand. What could Lester have done that was so bad that he'd sack Iris for letting him into the house? It doesn't make any sense."

"Aye, well..." Susan sighed. "There is a long history between 'em, an' it's best not to pry if you know what's good for you, Miss Viola. And that goes for you too, Bill...Bill?"

Bill was swaying and staring into space.

"Bill, are you all right?" Susan asked with concern. In the heat of the moment, Viola had forgotten all about her befuddled charge.

"I...I would like some water."

Thump!

Bill suddenly crumpled and hit the kitchen floor like a sack of spuds.

"Hell's teeth!" Viola exclaimed. "Take the skillet off the stove, Susan. You'll have to help me with him."

"Aye, all right, I'll help you get him back to bed, but I won't be much use otherwise. I'm no nurse."

Viola sighed. "Neither am I, Susan, but it's not like we can go and get the doctor now, is it?"

~III~

Blood and Glass

BILL NEVER WENT TO BOARDING SCHOOL. THE INJURY he suffered on that fateful day put him out of action for some considerable time and had a profoundly detrimental effect on his life. His personality changed almost overnight. He became sullen and withdrawn and was prone to violent mood swings. The once cheerful youth would snap and fly into uncontrollable fits of rage over the pettiest of reasons. It didn't help that the relationship between he and George had broken down almost immediately following the accident.

George finally visited Bill on his sickbed three days afterwards. He appeared in the room sometime after dark and stood in the corner just looking at Bill. His dazed and confused grandson hadn't noticed his entry and got a fright when he finally saw him. Lester had given Viola a tincture of laudanum for his pain and it had sent his brain to cuckoo land.

With a startled noise, Bill greeted his relative. "Um...Hello, Grandfather. I didn't see you there."

George didn't say a word, he just stood in the shadow-clad corner, watching him. In his time in Hollowhills, Bill could have counted the number of conversations between the two of them on one hand. George was the strong and silent type and spent a great deal of time down his precious mine, the archetypical "man of few words," but this was ridiculous.

"How are things? I feel like I've been here for weeks."

Still nothing. His eyes were just sunken pits of darkness and his lips were pursed.

"Grandfather...?" Bill was starting to get irritated by this point, so he decided to press a burning issue. "Why did you send Iris away?"

At this, George flinched, but still didn't respond. He was scrutinising Bill like he was looking for something. Like he was expecting to see *something*. A moment of painful silence hung in the air between them before George finally spoke. "Get well soon, William." He then turned and left, slamming the door behind him.

Bill was utterly perplexed. He knew that George was something of an "odd duck," as Susan put it, but this behaviour bordered on the unhinged. Something in his gaze had shaken him to the core, and then there was the fact that he had called him William—he hadn't used that since his father died. Before he could ponder too much over what had happened, Viola entered the room with a tray laden with his supper: soup with freshly-baked bread.

"How are we feeling tonight?" Viola asked cheerfully.

"Um…" Bill was still confused. "Not too good, Iris…"

"Viola."

"What?" Bill frowned.

"Viola. My name is Viola. You just called me Iris."

"Did I…? Sorry. I'm a bit confused. Grandfather was just here."

"Was he? That's nice. I don't mind saying that it's about time that he popped in to say hello." Viola placed the tray on the dresser and commenced sitting Bill up and propping him with lumpy feather pillows.

"He didn't." Bill sighed.

"Didn't? Didn't what?" Viola placed the tray in his lap and split the bread roll. The smell as it gently steamed was delightful. As much as she doted over Bill, she couldn't wait to get back down to the kitchen and consume her own repast.

"Didn't say hello, he just stood…in the shadows." An involuntary shudder went down his spine.

"What? Didn't he say anything?"

"He told me to 'get well soon,' that's all. Then he left. He seemed…*odd*."

"Yes, well." Viola perched herself on the foot of his bed and shook her head sadly. "He's been a little out of sorts since Iris left. I think it's all a bit too much for him. First your grandmother, then your father, and now her. He might pretend to be a man of iron, but I don't think he can cope. I think it's guilt that is doing it."

Bill lifted a soup-soaked hunk of bread to his lips and tried to avoid his stitches.

Viola patted his foot before standing. "I'll leave you to your supper. I'll check in later." And with that she left, leaving Bill alone with his thoughts.

What she had said made perfect sense. George *should* feel guilty about sending his housekeeper away. As he tucked into his soup, he tried to tell himself that his grandfather was just overcome with emotion and that he would snap out of it as soon as Bill recovered.

In that hope, Bill was sadly mistaken. This started a slow and steady decline, not just in their relationship, but in George's sanity. He was teetering on the edge of some kind of breakdown; it wouldn't take much to tip him over.

♎︎♏︎♎︎♌︎♎︎

Viola had been right about several things. George *was* upset about Iris leaving after the other tragedies, but she was wrong in one key respect. It wasn't guilt that nagged him. It was blame. George had stubbornly decided that he wasn't at fault in this scenario; he had been *forced* to get rid of her. She had gone against his wishes once again and let *that man* Lester into his home. This betrayal of trust simply couldn't be tolerated. No, he laid the blame squarely at Bill's shabby bedroom door. If he hadn't been such an idiot, none of this would have happened. In his increasingly troubled mind, Bill and Lester were somehow in league with each other. George wasn't at fault. George was the victim of a terrible conspiracy.

The fact that Bill became a regular patient of Lester's after the accident didn't help matters. Not that he had much choice. It was two weeks before Bill could get out of bed for any length of time. He suffered dizzy spells, chills, and bouts of violent nausea that would inevitably lead to blinding headaches that would have him wrapped up in blankets before one could say "chronic illness." This worried Viola immensely and she took it upon herself—without George's knowledge—to seek Lester's advice.

Dr. Lester proved to be surprisingly helpful in the matter. For a start, he instructed Viola how to remove the stitches when the time came and how to dress his wounds. He also gave her a little *something* to help Bill with his pain, a regular supply of laudanum and other pain medicines that would lead to a life-long dependency and his chosen profession.

Once he was up and about, the painful truth that he had missed his ticket out of Hollowhills came home to roost. Kirsten had been at his side almost continuously since she had returned from Penzance. Alas, her family member didn't last the week. Though she professed to feel bad that he hadn't left the village and pursued his dreams, she was a terrible liar and it was obvious to all—except Bill—that she was delighted. By now, she had moved into the draughty Conley home and was making the best of her role as housemaid. Bill made a show of being happy for her, but he too was a terrible liar. In reality, two things upset him about the situation: one, she couldn't look after him around the clock, and two, Tom Green had also got a position there as a stable lad. Though he was now sure that what he'd seen by the pond was a figment of his imagination, he couldn't help feeling the claws of the green-eyed-monster dragging sharply against his nether regions.

Six months passed before Bill was anything approaching his former self. Though he was still troubled by headaches and bouts of unfathomable rage, he managed, quite convincingly, to cultivate a facade that hid these undesirable character traits from the world. Even Kirsten was fooled into believing that he was well. Only two men knew any different: George and Dr. Lester.

As he had technically left the school and should have been away learning, Bill took it upon himself to self-educate using his grandfather's library. One afternoon, as he sat peering at the brown glass bottle containing the earthy liquid that he was becoming hooked upon, he found himself studying the label. It listed several ingredients that he had never heard of, so he turned to the index catalogue and sought out every possible book that he could find on the subject of pharmacology. From this, he decided that he would devote his time to study towards a medical career. Something that George was dead set against.

The increasingly erratic patriarch of the Johnson clan first got wind of Bill's plan when he was walking home from the mine early after something of a blackout. His workers had been pushed into tunneling deeper into the hills for some weeks and George had been with them every step of the way. One of the miners had taken ill that afternoon, which led to George going down to the deepest part of the mine. It was dark, humid, and cramped. Once there, George seemed to suffer some kind of seizure and both men had to be stretchered out. This was the start of many such *attacks* that George would go on to suffer before his end. To say he was surprised to see his grandson and Dr. Lester sitting outside the village pub would be a huge understatement. George was livid.

Pacing the library until Bill returned, George ambushed him as soon as he had taken his coat off. "Where the devil have you been?" he asked, knowing full well.

Bill was startled but managed to put on a remarkable show of indifference. "Oh, just out…taking some air, you know?" He finished with a smile, which was possibly the worst thing he could have done at that point.

"Liar!" George bellowed, turning a disturbing shade of red. "You were at the pub—with *him*."

Not at all intimidated, Bill retorted, "So what if I was? It so happens that I was asking his advice on an educational matter."

George gasped at his impertinence, his mouth working silently as he searched his mind for words. "Educational matter? What in blazes are you prattling about, boy?"

Smiling again, Bill proclaimed, "I am going to study to become a doctor, or at least a pharmacist. Isn't it marvelous?"

It was only now that George noted the faraway look on his grandson's face and his dilated pupils. "Have you been drinking?"

"Indeed!" Bill grinned. "I am well over thirteen, you know? It's quite legal."

"But, how? With what money?" George had images of the landlord appearing on his doorstep with a sizeable tab.

"Don't worry, Grandfather. Dr. Lester bought the drinks. He's quite good company, you know? I don't know why you hate him so." Bill was playing a dangerous game. He was playing up his intoxication to goad George into a full-scale row. He'd been spoiling for a fight for weeks and figured that now was as good a time as any.

Puffing and panting, George exploded. "Why? I'll tell you why. Because he's rotten to the core. Him and his *brotherhood*, but I got rid of most of them, sent them packing. There's only him and that damn fool Conley left in Hollowhills!" Realising he had said too much, George clamped his mouth shut and lashed out, punching the wall and bloodying his knuckles.

Bill flinched, suddenly this didn't seem like such a good idea. His relation's words and violent action worked him into a state of panic. "W-what a-are you t-talking about?"

George started to shake uncontrollably, his face turning purple.

"Tell me!" Bill screamed.

Viola and Susan burst in from the kitchen at the sound of the argument. "What the devil is going on here?" Viola demanded. She was becoming more and more like Iris with every passing day. "What's all this commotion?"

"I was just explaining to my *grandfather* that I'm to become a doctor, and Lester will be my tutor," Bill said with a sneer directed at George. "And there is nothing he can do about it, can you?"

Viola gasped.

Susan muttered obscenities.

George snarled and fixed Bill with a terrifying stare. All warmth and kindness had gone from his eyes, replaced by sheer malice and fury. "You will do as I say, William. For as long as you are under my roof, you will do as I say." A shadow flickered over his face, it was almost imperceptible, but Bill saw it clearly and nearly screamed. With his eyes clouding and turning black, George growled a warning, "There will be *consequences* if you don't do as I say," in such a menacing way that Bill was frozen to the spot. George balled his massive mitts and stepped towards Bill with violent intent. His voice sounded odd, somehow deeper and more cavernous. It reverberated around the entrance hall, bouncing off every painting and ornament.

Bill had gone too far. He had got the fight he was looking for and was about to pay for it in blood and broken bones. In his befuddled state, Bill hadn't considered the prospect of them actually coming to blows, but why would he? For all of his bluster, George had never once lain a finger on him. Now, however, it looked like he was going to break with tradition. Bill didn't stand a chance if it came down to it. George was taller, heavier, and far stronger than the younger man. Bill was about ten stone when sopping wet and couldn't punch his way out of a paper bag. Even if he'd been firing on all cylinders, which he wasn't, Bill would still have taken a pounding.

Anticipating a hammer-like blow, Bill shut his eyes, tensed his muscles, and prayed for it to be quick.

George abruptly stopped in his tracks, the colour draining from his cheeks. Shaking and jerking spasmodically, he clamped his hands to his ears, looked at Bill with a look of penitence and whispered, "forgive me...I tried..." before collapsing to the floor in an untidy bundle.

"Good grief!" Susan cried as she rushed to his aid. "Ee's had a funny turn."

Viola turned and glared at Bill. In all the years they had been together, he had never once seen *that* look on her face before: disappointment. "What the hell were you thinking? You know he's been under a lot of strain lately."

"I didn't mean to—"

"Just help us carry him to bed," Viola snapped, cutting him off.

"I just wan—"

"Enough!" Viola's eyes flashed with anger. "I've heard more than enough of your mouth for one day. Take his legs."

Doing as he was told, Bill helped the ladies carry his grandfather's bulk up to bed. It was a tense few hours before George recovered and came round. Once he was awake, he waved off his earlier *episode* and seemed to have little or no recollection of his set-to with his grandson. At least, that was what he claimed.

Bill had departed as soon as he was in bed and sequestered himself in the library. It was funny, he should have been feeling guilt after the altercation that led to George's collapse, but he didn't. Quite the contrary, in fact, he felt triumphant. Not only had he managed to stand up to him but he had also managed to get some information out of him. After flicking through the medical encyclopedias to find a diagnosis for George's condition and arriving at apoplexy, he turned his mind to the nuggets of information George had let slip about the mine and some kind of brotherhood.

As Viola was busy caring for George, and Susan had long since gone home, Bill took a draft of laudanum and crossed to his grandfather's desk. Feeling the frisson of the forbidden, he started to indulge in a spot of snooping. In his time at Hollowhills, he had never once dared pry into George's personal affairs. This was a transgression that would not be forgiven lightly. In his current mood, with opium and alcohol frolicking in his system, he didn't care one jot if he was caught.

The desk was a clutter of bills of sale, contracts, and other administrative minutiae that didn't interest him in the slightest. But, under a partially unfolded ordnance-survey-map, he struck tin. Next to a small pile of dusty old books was a ledger. Sitting down in George's chair, he started to flick through the pages. The majority of the entries were on business matters, but they seemed to trail off into wild ravings as they progressed.

The most illuminating of these entries were dated just three days previously:

Tuesday,

I've finally got rid of the last of the insidious brotherhood from my mines. It wasn't easy, but with help from Lucas, I managed to ferret him out. Now he is on a cart to Dartmoor Prison where he can join up with his comrades. Let them chant their blasphemies and light their candles in the comfort of their own cells. I will have to pay the magistrate a little bonus. His assistance in this matter has been invaluable.

This has come at a crucial time for me. My miners have finally broken through to the caverns beneath 'The Edge,' and who knows what rich pickings await us down there. I can ill afford to have Lester's cronies disrupt my men any more than they already have. If only I could get rid of Lester and Conley as easily. Those two monsters are a blight on our fair village, and could prove to be the downfall of us all.

I fear my grandson Bill may have fallen under Lester's influence. Whether Iris was intentional in her betrayal or not, she had to go. I miss her greatly, but I had little choice. Through her meddling, he may already be lost. I have seen the fire in his eyes, felt the heat of his rage. I have my suspicions that he may already be compromised. I should have tried harder to protect him. I did all I could.

Now, I must put on a mask of happiness and enjoy my dinner. After, I will slip away to my sanctuary and while away the evening in seclusion.

Reeling from the implications present in his grandfather's words, Bill closed the ledger and tucked it back under the map. Leaving the desk as he had found it, he wandered over to the drinks trolley and selected a glass.

"Let's see if this is as special as Grandfather says," he muttered as he uncorked a bottle of fine brandy and splashed two fingers into the glass. He had never tasted the stuff before, so he didn't know what to expect. The first gulp was a shock to the system; it burned his throat and made his stomach lurch. The second gulp was more of a soothing warmth that spread through his body. The third gulp was divine. Swirling the vintage libation in his glass, he settled into one of the comfy seats to savour its complex taste. Not soon after, Bill was asleep.

♎︎♋︎♓︎♏︎

Awaking with a start, Bill was surprised to find himself sitting in utter darkness. When he'd sat down, the waning light of dusk was still seeping through the windows. He hadn't dreamt, which was a mercy, so it felt as though he had merely closed his eyes for a second. His arms and legs felt like they had lead weights tied to them. It was similar to when he had awakened after his accident, but this time it was pleasurable. He felt serene and relaxed in a way that he hadn't since before his parents died.

Reaching for a candle and a box of Lucifer's matches, he sat up and lit the lamp. As the shadows receded around him, so did the calming atmosphere, replaced by a palpable feeling of tension and dread. Watching the candle flicker into life, Bill was sure that he heard a faint noise. It was almost like a low moan, as though the shadows were hurt by the light. Telling himself that he was still half asleep, he settled back into the seat.

Lester's tincture, along with the booze, made the flame look beautiful. The way it danced and swayed in the faint draft from the gap under the door was mesmeric and alluring. Bill watched it sway from left to right in a state nearing catatonia. As he watched the heat haze above the flame ripple the air, blurring and distorting the surroundings around the edges, Bill started to lose himself in the glow—that was when he heard whispering.

"W-who's there?" he yelped, snapping out of his trance. When nobody and nothing answered, he cocked his ear and listened. He could still hear the whispering. "Come on, Viola, is that you?"

Rising unsteadily, using the globe for support, he tried to listen for the source of the noise. It was then that he realised that it came from the flame itself. Leaning closer to the candle, he tried to hear what the flame was saying. It was whispering in a language not meant for human ears. Those blasphemous alien syllables chilled his soul and sent his blood racing through his veins in raging torrents. Losing his nerve, he blew out the candle.

In an instant, the shadows settled back into place and his mood returned to its previous joyful state. "It must be the brandy," he chuckled. "Come on, Bill. You're going as mad as that old fool upstairs."

Suitably convinced, he decided to take another glass of brandy up to his room and do some sketching. Leaving the library, he was surprised to see that it was just after twelve minutes past nine. He had dozed for around five hours. Smirking to himself, he mused that the night was still young. Changing his course, he slipped on his hat and coat, necked his brandy, and left the house, leaving the glass on the table in the hall.

Taking a lungful of the night air, Bill looked up at the moon and swayed. It was low and bulbous over the cave and mine riddled hills that gave the village its name. Looking past his family's mine towards the strange geological feature known as "The Edge," he was filled with images of hundreds of grubby miners toiling away like a colony of ants. He could almost hear the frantic bang and scrape of pick against rock as they searched for rich seams of metal. Vowing that he would never set foot down into that hellish place, Bill turned and looked towards Conley House.

Kirsten had a room in the main house overlooking the stables. There was a faint glow of light visible through the threadbare curtain indicating that she hadn't yet gone to sleep. Moving quietly to avoid arousing suspicion, he made his way along the road and hopped over the gate to the yard. From the noise in the stable house, it sounded like its occupants, Tom and Jack, were involved in a raucous drunken conversation. This was good; he shouldn't be disturbed.

Selecting a round pebble from one of Mrs. Gittings' rose beds, he positioned himself under Kirsten's window and took careful aim.

"And what the devil do you think you are up to, William Johnson?"

The acid tones of Mrs. Gittings made Bill leap into the air and nearly fall flat on his backside.

"Well?" Gittings had her arms folded across her chest. Her pinched face and tight weave of steel-grey hair brought to mind a grumpy old parrot as she tutted and fixed him with a look that could wilt begonias. "Explain yourself. I haven't got all day."

"Um...I..."

As Bill fumbled for words, Jack appeared in the doorway of the stable house. "Ah, there ye are, Bill. 'ave ye got that well water yet?"

"Um..."

"Oh, hello, Gittings." Jack flashed her a boozy grin, revealing his crooked yellow teeth. "Bill 'ere came to call on young Tom. Ye know, t' see if 'ee wanted to go down the pub. Tom ain't in a fit state though, 'ee's already hit the ale a bit too 'ard, so I sent Bill for some water...ain't that right, Bill?" Jack looked at him pointedly.

"Um...yeah, that's right. I was just going to the well." Bill smiled innocently.

Gittings harrumphed at the roguish odd-job-man. "Well, now you're here, he can go. Master Kenneth isn't well, as I'm sure you know. He doesn't need *visitors* prowling around his house at all hours of the night."

Bill wanted to point out that it wasn't even half-past-nine, but wisely held his tongue on the matter. "I'll be going then. Sorry to disturb you, Mrs. Gittings."

After she had tutted and turned to leave, Bill mouthed a silent "thanks" to Jack and followed her back to the gate.

Jack returned his gratitude with a wink and sloped off towards the well.

Reaching the gate, Bill briefly considered waiting for Gittings to go back inside the house and trying again, but quickly thought better of it. Gittings was bad enough, but if Kenneth Conley found him loitering outside his house, he would cop more than a tongue-lashing. The man's skill with a cane was legendary.

With a sigh, Bill looked towards his home and was preparing to head back when the front door of Conley House opened and Dr. Lester appeared on the doorstep. "Ah!" he exclaimed in surprise. "Bill, what are you doing here?"

Gittings was still lurking, so he had to be circumspect. "Just taking in the night air," he fibbed with a nod towards Kirsten's window.

Lester chuckled. "I see. Well, perhaps you would do me the favour of carrying these books?" He presented a small stack of ancient-looking texts. "It's going to be a struggle to carry them and my bag at the same time."

Bill smiled, glad of the invitation. After the day's events, he was more determined than ever to befriend the mysterious doctor. "Certainly. I'd be glad to."

"Come along, then." Lester handed him the books and led him down the crazy-paved path.

Gittings watched them leave with suspicion. Like Iris, she didn't trust Lester as far as she could throw him. Once they had closed the gate behind them, she made one final harrumph and went inside.

"You're dancing with death trifling with old Gittings." Lester chuckled. "That woman could put the wind up Lucifer himself. Do you know what the vicar calls her?"

"No."

"The Battleaxe of Bodmin Moor, that's what!" Lester broke into a loud chortle. "That wet blanket is absolutely terrified of the woman."

Bill chortled at this, then looked down at the books. The top-most appeared to be both ancient and in German. Bill frowned as he looked at the gold embossed title on the cracked leather binding. It proclaimed the book to be *Unaussprechlichen Kulten* by Friedrich Von Junzt. "Pardon me, Doctor, are these medical books?"

"No need to apologise, Bill. Curiosity is the key to knowledge. No, these books are of a *mystical* nature. Master Conley and I share interests in such matters."

"Is that what you were doing there…study?"

Lester sighed exasperatedly. "Alas, no. Kenneth has taken ill of late. Since he abandoned his teaching post and shut himself away from the world some years ago, he's been on something of a steady decline. He seems to be suffering from some kind of malady of the mind, the poor devil. I was there on medical, not personal, reasons, sadly. I fear he is finally losing his tenuous grip on reality. He has developed certain phobias that trouble him to the point of mania."

"Oh." Bill figured that it was good a time as any to broach the subject of his grandfather's outburst. "That must be a blow for you. Grandfather says that you two are close."

"Did he now?" Lester gave a lopsided smirk. "Yes. Kenneth and I are part of a *society*, you might say."

"Like the Freemasons?"

"Yes, you could say that, though our order is more of a brotherhood of like-minded thinkers. We prize knowledge over material wealth, unlike that glorified trader's guild."

"Brotherhood. Yes, that's what Grandfather called it."

"My, my, he has been loquacious. You can tell he wasn't himself. Normally you are lucky to get two syllables out of him, the miserable old goat. Did he say anything else?" Lester had a bemused grin plastered across his lips.

"Only that he'd got rid of some of your friends. I found a ledger, he mentions paying a magistrate to get them locked up. What had they done?"

Lester's face darkened. All mirth drained from his eyes. "Nothing, not a damn thing. He's paranoid, that's all. He has inherited *his* father's hatred of our brotherhood. Edgar Johnson was a member himself before he turned on my father."

"Why?"

Lester shrugged. "Who knows. A difference of ideals perhaps."

Bill went quiet and thought for a moment. Though he trusted Lester, something tickling the back of his mind told him that he wasn't telling him the whole truth.

Breaking the silence, Lester asked, "Do you think I could see that ledger?"

"Um, I..." Bill stuttered. Could he betray his kin to that degree? Would he align himself with his grandfather's rival, knowing that there was no going back? "Yes...I could sneak it over to you when he's down the mine."

"Excellent!" Lester beamed. "Well, here we are. Thank you for your help."

"It's nothing." Bill handed him the books and started to turn, but stopped and decided to ask the question that had been burning in his mind since his grandfather punched the wall. "How does one join your brotherhood?"

Lester smiled. "Why don't you come inside and have a brandy?"

As the door closed behind them, George sat up in his bed across the green and screamed.

ՇՑՇႶ

Bill and Dr. Lester talked long into the night. Most of what they discussed was about medical matters, though Lester did give him vague hints about his brotherhood. He would tell him more, he said, as his medical training progressed. The most important thing at that point was that he not let George know that they had discussed the matter. Lester feared, quite reasonably, that he would *get rid* of Bill the same way he *got rid* of the miners and Iris should he find out.

The two quickly formed a bond over the coming months. Bill did indeed sneak the ledger to his new pal one afternoon, much to Lester's delight. He painstakingly copied out the relevant passages, then let Bill take it back. George was none the wiser. Lester then sequestered the copies in his safe as insurance. Bill was worried that Lester would go to the law and that his betrayal would become common knowledge. Lester assured him that he would only do so if George's campaign against him intensified.

After a couple of weeks, Lester started to slip the odd *esoteric* text in with the medical books he loaned to Bill as part of his study. The first was a copy of Madame Blavatsky's *The Secret Doctrine*. He explained that, while mostly hokum, it did contain some of the basics of occult study that he would need if he was to join the brotherhood. Bill threw himself into both arms of his study. One of the side-effects of his lingering head injury was frequent bouts of insomnia. It didn't help that every time he closed his eyes, he saw his mother's mangled face.

The tincture of laudanum that Lester continued to prescribe was the only thing that would allow him to get any rest. His usage of the drug increased steadily, as did his use of alcohol. He had taken to stealing wines and spirits from his grandfather's well-stocked cellar and taking them up to his room. There, in seclusion, he would drink and dope himself to oblivion while he filled his head with all kinds of bizarre teachings.

After some of his heavier nights, he would find himself sketching the most abhorrent of things: giant amorphous creatures rising from the earth, cruel Egyptian-like gods inflicting tortures on slaves so despicable that they would have given the Marquis de Sade nightmares, and walls of living flame searing the flesh from the bones of man and beast. He would come to at dawn, with no knowledge of having drawn them and boggling at their hideousness. They were vivid in their ghastliness and he always made sure that they were well hidden by the time that Viola called him for breakfast.

Relations between Bill and George continued on their inexorable decline as they did their level best to give each other a wide birth. They would eat at different times and make doubly sure that the other was out when using the library. When he wasn't down the mine, George would be either locked away in his garden sanctuary or locked in the library. Viola and

Susan found the situation exhausting. Both women strived to mend the fences between the two to no avail. Neither man was willing to back down.

This carried on throughout the end of the year and into the spring of the following year where things finally came to a head.

♎︎♊︎♉︎♑︎

Awakening just before noon with a thick head from overindulgence, Bill rubbed his stinging eyes and looked down at the sketchbook in front of him. It was the same sketch that he had made a hundred times over recent years, the one of the garden with the shadow lurking on the boundary. It was the same in every exact detail, except the shadow was in the foreground staring up at him with one palm raised and a three-lobed eye in the centre of its head. On the shadow form's palm was a strange occult symbol.

Needles of phantom pain from the missing part of his finger jabbed into his nerves. Swearing and shaking his hand, Bill's mind raced back to that day. The day he first spilt his blood in that house. He saw the mantelpiece fall in slow motion. It tumbled and spun before landing with a sickening *crunch*. Then he saw the blood as it oozed from the mangled meat that had been his finger. Slowly, it spread onto the page from his sketchbook. It mingled with the charcoal rubbing, settling neatly into the lines and curves of the symbol on the hearth—*that* symbol. The very same symbol that the shadow figure had on its outstretched palm.

Clearly, George knew something about the figure that had somehow haunted Bill's dreams and dogged his footsteps since he arrived in Hollowhills. Why else would he have destroyed the symbol? Did he know what it meant? And if he didn't, had he done something incredibly foolish? Bill needed answers. He had read enough of Lester's books to know that one didn't just go around smashing wards, runes, and glyphs willy-nilly. He closed his sketchbook and got dressed. It was time for George to talk, but first, he would go and speak to Dr. Lester.

Lester had spent most of the afternoon with Kenneth Conley. The old recluse's sanity was hanging by a thread. Mrs. Gittings had reluctantly sent for him to administer a sedative. Over the years, Conley had developed an acute fear of mirrors. That morning, however, Gittings found him staring into one, holding a candle while rambling in a strange dialect. Fearing for his sanity, she had marched across the green and gave Lester's door a knocking that could have awakened the dead.

Finding a note addressed to him informing him of Lester's whereabouts, Bill killed time by visiting the pub with some coins he had pilfered from George's desk. Once he had a beverage in his mitts, he perched on the wooden bench out front and tried to relax. Sitting alone, sipping porter, he watched the sleepy village go through its daily change. The afternoon sun slowly sank behind the hills, ushering in shadows that changed the entire complexion of the place. It went from picturesque to sinister in under an hour.

Finally, the door of Conley House creaked open like a gaping mouth and spat Lester onto the path. Bill watched as he made his way to the road with Mrs. Gittings' rapier-like eyes stabbing into his back. Bill chuckled to himself. There was something distinctly comical about how the old guard of the village viewed Dr. Lester. He mused that it was because they distrusted medical science and would have been happier with leeches and eye-of-newt than with modern methods.

Draining the remainder of his third flagon, he stood and jogged over the green to meet his mentor.

"Hello there, Bill," Lester called out in greeting. "Careful you don't slip in that mud."

"How's Conley?" Bill panted, drawing level with the doctor.

"Not good, I'm afraid. He's in the grip of some kind of brain fever. I'm no alienist, but I would have him committed to an asylum if he wasn't a friend. I will have to get you inducted into the brotherhood quicksticks or I'll be the only one left in the village at this rate."

Bill frowned, something about Lester's manner was off. Despite the direness of his words, he seemed more excited than worried. "Sorry to hear that," he muttered sombrely. "Have you sedated him?"

"I have given him some of my special tincture, the one you use, to soothe his nerves. I'll be heading back over once I've mixed up some more."

"Oh, you make it yourself?" This was news to Bill.

Beaming with pride, Lester replied in the affirmative. "Indeed. It's an old recipe I came across in my study, with a few modifications for modern ingredients, you understand? It was used by Druids and mystics as far back as the Roman occupation, and if it was good enough for the Druids, it's good enough for us!"

Bill had never seen Lester so animated. It wasn't just the talk of his *special* medicine that had him enthused neither. Something else was whipping him into a state of excitement. Bill chose to cut their meeting short as, for the first time, he was becoming distinctly uneasy in Lester's presence. "Um…I won't keep you. I just wanted to ask you something, if I may?"

"Ask away, my boy, ask away!" Lester's eyes twinkled in the dusk light.

"Well," Bill began, hurriedly sidestepping a large pile of dog mess, "do you recall what I told you about my dreams?"

"The ones about your parents and the *shadow*?"

"Well, I've been sketching, how shall I put it? Under the influence."

Lester chuckled at this. "How bohemian! You'll be writing poetry next. Sorry, do go on."

"*Ahem*, yes, well… A lot of them contain the shadow-man. I drew one last night that showed him to have a symbol on his right hand. It was the exact same symbol that I found on the hearth when my finger was crushed."

Lester flinched at the memory. He had seen the piece of paper with the rubbing and the blood. "Really? That is odd."

"It gets worse. The day after the accident, I found my grandfather in a funny old state, he had smashed the tile from the hearth and destroyed the symbol—"

"What?" Lester exploded, catching Bill off guard. "The fool! The bloody fool! That symbol was a protective sigil…" He trailed off, staring into space and muttering to himself. "That would explain… Oh, the meddling fool."

"Dr. Lester?" Bill shook him by the shoulder. "What is going on?"

Lester blinked, his face returning to its normal genial expression. "I'm sorry, I'm sure it's nothing to worry about. Now, if you would excuse me, I must crack on." With that abrupt ending to their conversation hanging in the air, Lester turned back towards his house and hurried away, leaving Bill standing in the middle of the green with his mouth wide open.

♑︎♋︎♉︎♒︎◻︎

"Ah, there you are, Bill," Viola sighed when Bill entered the house. "George has been looking for you. He seemed in a foul mood."

"Oh, why?" Bill asked distractedly.

Viola folded her arms across her chest the same way Iris used to before she handed out a tongue lashing. "It may have something to do with all the empty bottles you had hidden in the coal bunker. He's furious that you have been helping yourself to his libations."

"Ah…" Bill waved it away. "I'll replace them when I become a doctor." Bill mounted the stairs.

"He's just popped out to see his foreman, Lucas. He wants to talk to you when he gets back. He said he'll be an hour or two. I'll call you when he's home."

George wanted to *talk*? This wasn't good at all. Bill gulped before affecting an air of nonchalance. "Thank you, Viola. I shall be in my chambers."

Shaking her head in exasperation, she called after him, "Go easy on the laudanum. You will need a clear head." When he didn't reply, she tutted under her breath and went back into the scullery to continue her chores.

Three hours passed before Viola appeared. During which time, he actively rebelled against her advice and imbibed a massive dose of his medicine to keep the nagging headache and the whispering voices behind his eyes at bay. After his talk with Lester, he had been far too discombobulated to focus on his medical study and had instead immersed himself in sketching the symbol from the hearth. As he linked the lines and curves and the oddly shaped eye appeared, there was a definite shift in the shadows. They seemed to hum and vibrate as though alive.

Taking the Davy lamp from the bedside table, he lifted the gauze to brighten the light. The shadows almost seem to try to resist the light for a fraction of a second, but eventually receded. Telling himself that he was imagining things, he placed the exposed lamp on the dresser and finished his sketch. Once it was done, he leaned back in his chair and awaited his summons. As it turned out, he didn't have that long to wait.

Viola led him down the stairs like the condemned going to the gallows. Neither of them said a single word as they went their separate ways at the bottom. Viola went into the drawing room and Bill walked slowly towards the kitchen. Despite his bravado, he was dreading this showdown. Stopping outside the door, he took a deep breath to steady his nerves before opening the door and stepping inside.

George was hunched over his desk as he had been on that first day. He didn't look up from his ledger when Bill entered. It was a wonder that smoke didn't come off his dip-pen, he was scribbling so furiously. Bill cleared his throat to grab his attention. "You wanted to see me, Grandfather?"

George stopped writing and placed the pen down on a clump of blotter paper. If Bill was expecting fire and fury, he was to be disappointed as, for now, his grandfather was calm and collected. George smiled and indicated the chair opposite the desk. "Please, sit." He paused while Bill got comfortable before continuing. "It has come to my attention that you have been drinking quite heavily of late. I understand that you have been through a lot, but if you are determined to drink yourself into oblivion, that's your prerogative, but I will not fund your habit any longer."

Bill began to argue but was silenced by a raised finger.

"Pray, let me continue. You are my grandson and despite our differences on certain *matters—*"

"Dr. Lester," Bill interjected.

"Quite. Look, you are my flesh and blood, and I care for you deeply, but I will not have a parasite stealing my money, drinking all my vintage brandy, and eating me out of pocket." He suddenly rose and slapped his ledger with the flat of his hand. "You need to earn a wage, my boy! And, to that end, I have arranged with my second in command, Lucas, to get you trained in mine management. I'm not in the rudest of health, as I'm sure you have noticed, and I need someone to take the reins when I'm gone."

"But!" Bill rose to argue, but George cut him off.

"No arguments. It's either that or you find someone else to sponge off. I've had it with your nonsense. You need to grow up and become a man, William Johnson!"

Bill was distraught; this was the last thing in the world he wanted to hear. "I will NOT work in your filthy mines! I am to become a doctor, and that is final!"

"Balderdash!" George exploded, turning that scary shade of purple again. "Sitting up in your room, drugged to the eyeballs, reading that occult rubbish, is not becoming a damn doctor. Maybe your *friend* would be a better doctor himself if he swapped those abhorrent tomes for the *Medical Gazette* once in a damn while."

Bill's blood was starting to boil. For some reason, it was the slight on his friend and mentor that hurt more than the personal barbs. The rage was returning as the shadows closed in and the buzzing started to build from the pits of his stomach. "You know nothing about Lester, you old fool!"

"What?" George snapped, swiping a stack of books off his desk. "How dare you!"

"You heard me. If you gave him a chance in the first place, instead of holding onto your father's prejudice, maybe I wouldn't hate you as I do!"

This was like a slap to George's face; he wobbled and steadied himself on the desk.

"You're a hateful man, George Johnson, a hateful man and a pig-headed oaf. You proved that when you got rid of Iris!"

Another verbal slap.

The buzzing in Bill's ears was almost deafening and his voice rose accordingly. "You said about my books… What about your ledger? Hmm? What about those miners you set up?"

George slumped into his chair, stammering and fighting for breath. "H-how dare—"

"Enough! You talk of Lester's brotherhood, but your father was a member, wasn't he? You knew about that symbol on the fireplace, didn't you? What do you know about the shadow?"

"I-I don't—"

"Lies! All you say to me is lies! What can you tell me about *this*…" Bill whipped the sketches of the strange eye symbol from his pocket and shoved it under George's downturned face.

George flung his head back and slammed into the back of his chair with such force that he nearly demolished it. "Get it away!" George shrieked. "Get that *thing* away from me!"

Shadows were clouding Bill's vision as his body started to shake uncontrollably. The buzzing was overwhelming by this point and was suddenly joined by another, more disturbing sound—the voice of the shadow.

Finish him, Will, William, Willy… He's almost done… Finish him off, Bill, Billy!

Bill smirked viciously and stepped towards his stricken grandfather. "You can't take the truth, can you?" He sneered and prepared to unleash another tirade.

Before he could let rip, Viola burst into the room. "What in the hell? Bill, what are you playing at?"

Bill snapped his head in her direction, his muscles were so tense that there was an audible *crack*. Viola blanched away from the look in his eyes but held her ground. "Can't you see that he's unwell?"

George did indeed seem to be in the grip of some kind of attack. His eyes were rolling and he was hyperventilating.

"Out! Now!" Viola screamed.

Bill moved towards her menacingly, but she refused to be intimidated and pointed her finger towards the door. "Out!"

Growling in the back of his throat, Bill took the hint and stormed past her out of the library and out towards the kitchen.

Seek the truth... Embrace the shadow... Set me free.

The kitchen was in complete darkness that washed over him. It made him feel powerful, alive. Cracking his knuckles and snarling through gritted teeth, he looked for something to smash. Violent rage had flared up inside him, building pressure and approaching critical mass. If he didn't unleash his fury soon, he would explode.

"I'll just tend to your precious conifers, Grandfather," he hissed, with spittle flecking his lips.

Don't waste your time on trees... Prune the deadwood in the library...

Trying to ignore the inner voice and steer his hands away from Susan's razor-sharp knives, he slammed through the back door, nearly taking it off its hinges. Breaking into a run, he hastened to the top garden with his vision narrowing and the buzz intensifying. This time he wouldn't just be using the axe handle, he was fixing to attempt some amateur tree surgery.

Reaching the tool shed, Bill bellowed in fury to see a thick padlock barring his entry. George had kept it locked up as tight as a duck's backside since his last explosion. Refusing to be denied his catharsis, he searched around for a suitably large rock to smash the lock off with.

Moving towards the lean-to at the rear of the sheds, Bill yelped in shock as he caught sight of his reflection in the glass. Weak moonlight had given him a cadaverous appearance and his eye sockets were sunken and dark. The image of his drowned father, as seen in his dreams, flickered in front of his face. With a cry of sorrow and anger, he lashed out with his right hand, shattering his reflection.

The grimy plate glass, brittle with age and exposure to the elements, fractured into several jagged shards. One of the larger pieces fell like the blade of a guillotine, slamming into the back of his hand. Blood showered the interior of his grandfather's rough construction as Bill let out a primal roar of pain.

Grabbing his hand and falling against one of the conifers, he pulled the glass clear of his flesh. Luckily, the shard had remained intact and hadn't splintered on impact. The wound was a perfect line just below the knuckles that stretched from index to pinkie. His blood, thinned by the alcohol in Lester's tincture, flowed in a steady stream that dripped onto the mud at his feet.

Don't waste it...use it... Feed me...make me stronger...

Stumbling out from behind the lean-to, Bill lurched around to the front of George's sanctuary, dipped a finger in his sticky fluid, and started to paint the eye symbol on the door. Each completed line caused a sharp *crack* to echo in his cranium. It was accompanied by flashes of strange images of a lightless tomb, a rolling desert, a toppled faceless statue, and finally, the debilitating light of an everlasting flame. When the final line was complete...the flame was extinguished.

Good, good...I am nearly free... Feed me more blood...

"I have no more to give," Bill wailed, sinking to his knees.

Then, give me the blood of another...

Shaking and sweating, Bill tore off his shirt and wrapped it around his injured hand. "No! I won't!" Finding the strength within himself to refuse, he curled up in a ball in the mud as the voice howled in the darkness of its now Stygian prison. Assaulted by flickering images of human sacrifice and depraved acts of worship at the feet of a Sphinx with a seething mass of tentacles for a face, Bill lapsed into unconsciousness.

♅☥♄

"Master Bill. Come on, for God's sake, wake up!" Susan's words cut through Bill's drugged slumber like an axe. Each shrill syllable dug into the space behind his eyes like a surgical scalpel, twisting and gouging.

Bill groaned and opened his eyes. The harsh morning light burned his retinas, as the twin fuzzy images of the distressed-looking cook merged into one solid whole.

"Oh, thank the Lord! I thought we'd be burying two o' you at this rate."

"Wha-what…?" Suddenly alert, Bill slowly pulled himself to his knees. He was in a terrible state, bare-chested and caked in blood and dirt. "What do… What do you mean, *two*?"

"I'm sorry, Bill." Susan started to weep, her broad shoulders heaving. "I 'ave some terrible news. Your grandfather died sometime last night. Viola just found 'im slumped over 'is desk in the library, cold as stone, 'ee was."

Bill could see in Susan's eyes that she was anticipating more than a bewildered grunt at this bombshell, but his brain was so mangled by the combined shock of the news and the laudanum hangover that he couldn't get his mouth to work. His jaw hung slack and his eyes drifted.

Susan gasped upon seeing his ripped and bloodied hand. Grasping him by the shoulders, she dragged him over to the shed and propped him against the wall. He was positioned directly under his sigil of blood as she peeled away his makeshift bandage and peered at the gaping wound. Her lips were moving up and down as she tried to get a message through his brain fog, but it was no use; Bill was on an entirely different plain, one of menacing shadows and dark entities. Entities that wanted into our world—by any means necessary.

"Use the rainwater in the butts to clean yerself up, for God's sake. I'll fetch ye a clean shirt. Viola is in enough of a state without you rolling in lookin' like ye've just got back from the war," Susan scolded him as he finally managed to banish the haunting whispers and buzzing sounds to the back of his mind and actually hear her.

"Ugh, thanks…" Leaning over, he cupped his hands in the chill water that had been collected in an old metal drum. The icy droplets went some way to revive him and it was only now that the reality of the situation came to the fore. His grandfather was dead. After a blazing row that left him gasping for air, George Johnson had died.

"Sorry, Grandfather…"

Alone with his thoughts, Bill knew that he was at least partially responsible, but he didn't seem to care. He felt no remorse or sorrow, he felt nothing. He was completely numb. Dazed and utterly confused.

After each of his *episodes*, the buzzing in his head had disappeared after he had come out of it. Not this time. It was still there, tickling at the back of his brain. His pineal gland had been touched by something from *outside.* It had become a receiver, picking up transmissions and feeding their messages into his epithalamus. The act of daubing that symbol in his own blood had opened his third eye. It was wide open—and watching.

Bill's contemplative reverie was broken by Susan rustling through the rose arch with a clean shirt and Dr. Lester in tow. She had a face like thunder and chucked the shirt at him before huffing off back to the kitchen.

"My, my, you have been in the wars, haven't you?" Lester sighed as he placed his bag on the ground and retrieved his needle and thread. He seemed agitated and deflated, which struck Bill as odd. Surely, he should have been elated? His rival and main detractor had shed his mortal coil and he was now free to enter the house, so why the fraught expression and haunted look?

"Hello…Doctor…" was all Bill managed to slur in response.

"What the devil were you up to?"

"I…I lost my temper again. The shadow…the shadow made me do things."

Lester's eyes fixed on Bill's, they were wide and filled with fear. "What *things*?"

Bill pointed up to the blood sigil with his free hand. "I lost control."

Upon seeing the sign, Lester's terror deepened, though he did a damn fine job of concealing it. Feigning disinterest, he smiled. "Oh, is that all? I thought for one moment that you had killed George, though I'm pretty sure he has had a stroke. The post-mortem will confirm it, I'm sure."

Grabbing Bill's head, he pulled apart his eyelids and peered at his dilated pupils. "As I suspected," he said with a shake of his head. "How much of the medicine did you take last night?"

"Um—"

"However much it was, it was too much," Lester cut him off. "You will have to be more careful in future, it's a potent tincture." He returned to stitching Bill's hand as his voice took on a sombre tone. "I'm afraid we both suffered a loss last night."

"What? What do you mean?"

"I'm afraid, that at approximately the same time your grandfather died, Kenneth Conley also passed from the mortal realm." Lester's face betrayed feelings of both anger and sadness, but Bill didn't notice either. His head was spinning with the news.

"I'm sorry, I know you were close. How's Kirsten?" Despite how close they had been, Bill hadn't spared his potential mate a single thought in what seemed like weeks. He had been so wrapped up in his own little world that he had practically forgotten all about her.

"A little shaken. She was the one who found him conked out in his study."

The similarity between the two deaths wasn't lost on Bill, but he chose to sidestep the issue. "What will happen to the house?"

"I'm not sure. I believe that it will go to his only surviving relative, a nephew that currently resides in Truro. He's a fellow medical man. I'm expecting him to contact me soon regarding the burial. I'm sure that Kirsten will find another position if needs be."

"Yeah." Bill winced as Lester poured alcohol on the freshly sewed up laceration.

"There. Not my neatest work, but it will suffice. Come on, let's get you inside."

Grabbing Lester's proffered hand with his uninjured one, Bill rose and grabbed onto the shed for dear life while his legs came back to life. Slipping on the shirt and buttoning it, he looked towards the house. "This isn't going to be fun."

"No, it certainly isn't. I'll be over at my abode should you wish to join me for a brandy later. We should talk about your *episodes*."

"Wait…you're not coming in with me?"

Lester chuckled dryly. "I most certainly am not. I've had quite enough of Susan and Viola for one morning, clucking at me like a pair of broody hens. I've already had to deal with a distraught Mrs. Gittings, I've suffered more than enough for one day. Besides, I want to check some books in my study for—" He stopped himself short and smiled. "Well, let's just say, I have some things I want to go over. About the deaths, you understand?"

"Um, yes, I understand. I'll see you later then?"

Lester nodded curtly before leaving via the side entrance. Bill stood in the centre of the lawn and looked at the house. *His* house now, presumably. Lester was right to make himself scarce. Bill wished he could have joined him. He was going to need that brandy later.

~IV~

Fire and Revelation

"I FEEL STUPID."

"No reason to feel stupid, Bill. Just stare into the flame." Lester had positioned a fat tallow candle on the desk in his study and had positioned his *patient* in front of it. "Watch how it dances. See the shimmer, the haze, the radiance. Feel the heat coming off it. Clear your mind so all you can see is the flame. All you can hear is the ticking of the clock."

The week following the funerals of George Johnson and Kenneth Conley, Bill retreated to Lester's home to escape the accusatory stares of his cook and housekeeper. Though neither woman said as such, he could see it in their eyes that they held him at least partially to blame for his grandfather's death—and, in a way, they were right. He didn't blame himself, however, he blamed an external force. The *shadow* that had been whispering in his ear ever since he spilled his blood on the strange symbol on the hearth.

As they had sat and sipped brandy in contemplation, Bill had detailed every significant event and *episode* since arriving in Hollowhills leading up to the previous evening's rage and drug-induced stupor. Lester had tried to hand-wave most of it away as being the effect of his head injury and the drugs, but he was an unconvincing liar. Bill told him as such, so Lester drip-fed him just enough information to sound plausible.

Lester explained that his great-grandfather had founded a cult to further his mine business. In return for their worship and compliance, the Johnson family and their cronies would gain power and wealth. He went on to explain that this was why their families had fallen out. His brotherhood was dedicated to keeping the shadow in the light. It was now that he finally revealed the full title of his organisation: The Brotherhood of the Flame.

As much as Bill wanted to dismiss this tale as claptrap, the evidence was too great to ignore. Unbelievable as it sounded, George Johnson was a cultist!

"We're approaching twelve minutes past nine. This gives us the number thirty-three, which, in numerological terms, means communication. What I want you to do is think about the shadow. When I ring this bell, I want you to picture the shadow in your mind's eye. Nod if you understand."

Bill nodded, his face wearing a bemused expression.

Ding-a-ling-a-ling!

Screwing his eyes tightly shut, Bill pictured the shadow as it had last revealed itself. He pictured it lurking in the tree line. The heat of the flame became more intense. He pictured the shadow raising its hand. The flame started to hiss. He pictured the shadow open its hand and display the symbol—

Woosh!

Bill's eyes snapped open as the flame burst from the wick and formed into a roiling incandescent orb. "What the hell is that?" he screamed as he tipped backwards in his chair and clattered to the floor.

Lester didn't reply. His eyes were rolled back in his head and his lips were moving as he mouthed a silent incantation.

Rolling onto his front, Bill sprung to his feet. "Dr. Lester, what the hell is that thing?"

Wispy tendrils like the fronds of anemones burst from the orb and started to grope for Bill's face. He backed away, looking for something to defend himself with. The only thing close to hand was a vase stuffed with several limp daffodils. He grabbed the stems and threw them at Lester's head before tossing the water into the orb.

A gout of superheated steam billowed from the centre of the sun-like creature as Bill dived under Lester's antique desk whimpering in fright.

"What the hell did you do that for?" Lester exclaimed as his eyes rolled back the right way around and the orb shrank and became a flame once again. "You bloody fool! He was nearly free!"

"What?" Bill slowly crawled out from his hiding place. "Who was nearly free? What the hell was that *thing*?"

"Thing? How dare you call it a *thing*, that was a god!" Lester raged. "I was so close this time…so damn close! And you, you ruined it!"

"Ruined it? It nearly killed me!" Bill fired back, his fear turning to anger.

"You would have been cleansed!" Lester screamed in manic exultation, his hands raised to the roof, sweat pouring from his forehead.

Bill edged past him to the door. "You're bloody mad! You're just as insane as my grandfather!" Fearing for his life, he bolted from the room.

It took a second for Lester to snap back to reality. When he did, he was aghast. "No, wait!" he called after his fleeing protégé. "I'm trying to save you! I'm trying to save us all!"

"Stay the hell away from me!"

Slam!

The house shook from the force at which Bill slammed the door behind him as he raced into the night.

"Fool!" Lester spat. "After all the time and effort I've put in. After everything I have given him..." he sighed and slumped into his chair. "Oh well, there is one more person I can use. My god *will* be freed!" As he roared the final words, he thumped the desk in determination. Dr. Lester was not beaten yet—not by a long shot.

♌♍♎♏

Hit by the night air and free from the lick of Lester's insidious flame, Bill took a couple of deep breaths and looked up at the fat gibbous moon lurking over the mine. The mine—that would be his now as well. He cursed under his breath. Yet more hassle that his grandfather had burdened him with. Still, it meant that he would have money coming in, and money meant booze and medicine.

The back of his head started to tingle and his pineal gland became active. Slowly turning back in the direction of Lester's house, he gave a start to see the demented practitioner peering at him from the window with blazing eyes and a disturbing rictus grin etched into his sallow features. Returning his gaze, Bill flipped him a rude hand gesture and stalked off towards his home.

Pausing just before the gate, the terror of the situation finally hit home. He was seemingly stuck in the middle of two warring factions of insane occultists. Was he just a pawn in a game he couldn't comprehend? He had thought Lester eccentric, but utterly benign. It appeared that he had been wrong, and that his grandfather had been right to warn him about the man. Now the guilt kicked in. Now he felt wretched.

Was the shadow something to do with his grandfather? Was this just another deception? One thing was for sure, what Lester had conjured in his study *was* evil. He could feel the malevolence sparking off it. Feel its hateful gaze as it attempted to sear his flesh and burn out his mind. There was no way in hell that it was anything but evil.

All these questions, doubts, and emotions were too much for him to bear. Reaching into his coat pocket, he took one of the brown bottles that Lester had prepared for him, unstopped the neck, and took a gulp. The laudanum surged down his throat and hit his stomach like a sledgehammer. He knew from the very instant he tipped his head back to swallow that it had been too much. There were still enough opiates from the previous few days in his system to sedate a walrus and combined with the several brandies he had imbibed over the past few hours, it was a recipe for disaster.

A brief moment of panic was dispelled by a shrug of the shoulders as the medicine worked its magic on his nerves. "It'll be fine. Nothing to worry about." He grinned inanely as the gate started to warp and twist away from his tremulous grasp. Eventually grabbing hold of it, he opened it and nearly went flat on his face on the path. Plunging towards the door, he grabbed the wall for dear life as he tried to steer his key into the lock. It took far longer than it should have to unlock the door and even longer to navigate the doorstep.

Finally making it inside, he careered into the library and collapsed on the leather couch.

Colours and shapes crackled over his eyes every time he blinked, then lingered in his vision as he stared up at the ceiling. In a state of numbness, he watched the shadows cast by the sickly yellow moonlight streaming through the window dance on the ceiling. It was then that he had an epiphany. He had to get away from Hollowhills. Things were lurking behind the picturesque facade that no human mind should ever have to confront, and he had the disturbing feeling that he had barely scratched the surface. To find out that his grandfather was a member of a cult was bad enough, but to then discover that his friend and mentor was a madman willing to feed him to a sentient fireball was too bizarre for words.

Once his grandfather's will had been settled, Bill would surely inherit a sizeable estate. If he sold the house and the mine, he would accrue a small fortune. It would be more than enough to set him up financially. His spirits began to soar as he pictured a nice little townhouse in one of the more progressive cities. Nothing ostentatious, but somewhere he could entertain polite society. Yes, as soon as the funeral was taken care of, he would put things into motion and finally escape from that wretched village.

You cannot leave.

Bill let out a warbling cry as two sharp daggers of pain stabbed into his temples. Squirming in agony, he twisted and fell off the couch, landing with a *thump* that drove the air from his lungs. Gasping and writhing across the floor like a beached sea slug, Bill crawled towards his Grandfather's drinks trolley. Maybe a brandy would clear his head?

There is no escape for you…

"Get out of my head!" Crawling up the side of the desk, he suddenly came face-to-face with the cadaverous form of George, sitting behind his desk, his eyes two voids of shadow.

"You can't escape…" George sneered, his voice like the creak of a coffin lid. "Embrace the shadow… Let it inside!" His rigour Mortis twisted hands reached for Bill's face as his mouth opened wide, nearly bisecting his face. "Join with me!" Inky smoke started to flow from his open maw as his tongue thrashed around like a bloated grave worm.

"Argh! Keep away! You're dead, you're bloody dead! You can't be walking!" The library pitched on its side as he backed into the drinks trolley. Fine crystal decanters and glassed tinkled to the floor in a deafening *crash*. The room revolved around him as he tumbled to the floor, overturning a stack of well-thumbed books on mining that skidded across the polished wooden boards.

"Bill! What the hell are you doing?" Viola suddenly appeared at the door with a mixture of concern and irritation on her face. She had aged so very quickly over the past few years. For a disconcerting second, Bill was convinced that it was Iris at the door.

"G-Grandfather!" Bill babbled, backpedaling and slamming his hand down onto shards of broken glass. His blood started to flow into the fabric of the house yet again. "He...he wants me to give my soul to the shadow! God, Viola, don't let it take me!"

Startled by his nonsensical words, she rushed across the room and crouched next to him, cooing softly. "It's all right, Bill. There is nothing to fear. Nothing's going to hurt you."

Looking around frantically, Bill breathed a relieved sigh to see that his grandfather was nowhere to be seen. "I...I must have nodded off. Bad dream." His words were thick and glutinous, like he had a mouthful of toffee.

Viola noticed his drugged state and peered into his eyes. He was completely away with the faeries. Shaking her head and tutting, she looked at him in dismay. "How much laudanum have you taken?"

Viola gasped as Bill raised his hand to indicate a small measure with his thumb and forefinger. Blood from a multitude of small lacerations started to run down his palm and onto his shirt cuff.

"Oh, Lord! You're bleeding, again. Wait there, I'll go and fetch Dr. Lester."

"No!" Bill snapped to full awareness. "You'll do no such damn thing, woman!"

"I beg your pardon?" She was both irate and bewildered; the two had been practically inseparable since George passed away.

"Sorry, Viola. I…I just don't want *that* man in my house."

"What? I don't understand."

"Grandfather was right."

"But, you need to get patched up."

Bill looked at the wounds and shrugged. Though there were many, they weren't deep. "It'll be fine. fetch me some bandages, a needle and thread. I can do it myself."

"Fine." Viola threw up her hands in exasperation and hurried towards the door.

"Oh, Viola?"

She stopped and fixed him with a questioning expression.

"Fetch a bottle of brandy from the cellar, will you?"

"Don't you think you've had enough?" Viola's tone was as sharp as a lemon.

Bill could barely mask the irritation in his voice. "It's for the cuts."

Folding her arms across her bosom and raising an eyebrow, she replied in a sarcastic tone, "Really?"

Bill's voice cracked like thunder as his temper once again snapped. "Just fetch it, damn you!"

Viola turned white and muttered some deeply unladylike words in his direction before nodding curtly and leaving the room.

"How dare she!" Bill was furious. The pain in his head was subsiding, only to be replaced by an electrical tingle at the back of his head. "Who does she think she is?" The buzzing was building from his pineal gland and slowly filling his auditory canal.

Using the bookcase as a ladder, Bill hauled himself upright and wobbled backwards, jabbing his rump on the corner of his late grandfather's desk. Pain shot from his coccyx all the way up his spinal column and into his head, amplifying whatever signal his conarium was picking up and making his arms spasm and jerk.

Viola had left an exposed lamp on the desk when she had entered and the brilliance of the light scything into his bloodshot eyes added more galvanizing agony to the mix.

"Curse that woman!" He scowled as he slammed the guard down, extinguishing the flame.

Teach her a lesson, Bill, Billy, Will, Willy… Teach her not to play with fire.

The library was lit only by the dim light from the gas jet by the door. The darkness pulled in around Bill, wrapping him in its grasp, seeping into his pores, invading his heart. The wavering light only afforded a small circumference of illumination that struggled to keep the dark at bay. Bill smiled as the presence in his head muttered foul things and implanted seeds of hideous tortures and depraved acts into his mind's eye.

I need blood… Feed me her soul… Let me inside.

As his hand tightened around a silver letter-opener, Bill suddenly realised what was happening and launched it across the library. "No! I won't hurt her!"

You cannot resist…surrender to me…

"Get out of my head, curse you. Get out of my damned head!"

"Bill? Who are you talking to?"

He hadn't noticed that Viola had returned and

jumped as her voice cut through the chaos in his head. She stood in the cone of light. It reflected off her white apron giving her an almost angelic glow. It was so intense that he had to shield his eyes from the glare. "Um...n-nobody."

"Are you sure you don't need me to fetch the doctor?"

"No! I don't need *his* help." He took three steps towards her but stopped at the edge of the light and grabbed his head in agony. The stabbing pain had returned with a vengeance.

"That's it! I'm getting the doctor. You're not well!"

"Stop meddling!" Bill screamed above the noise in his head. "All you ever do is meddle. I will not have you interfering anymore. Get out before I—" As he took another step towards Viola, his legs buckled and his eyes rolled back into his skull as he collapsed to the floor and bounced his head off the wood. Everything went dark once again.

♎︎♓︎♎︎

Come and find me...

Bill found himself lying on wet grass in the precincts of a decrepit Catholic church. His head was resting on a granite slab, which could have explained the pain in his head, had he not been dreaming. "Wha-what the hell is this place?" Sitting up, he scrutinized the bent and crooked spire. The cross at the apex was blackened as though it had been recently struck by lightning. Slates had fallen to the graveyard below, leaving a gaping hole in its side.

The spire was backlit by a high moon that highlighted the shadows and gave it a skeletal aspect. Getting slowly to his feet and steadying himself on a teetering tombstone, Bill scanned the graveyard for some kind of clue to his whereabouts. One thing was for sure, he wasn't in Cornwall anymore.

A large black rat shot from a hole caused by dislodged bricks on one of the tabletop tombs carrying what looked like a finger bone in its teeth. Bill jumped to his feet and backed away, fearing more of its fellows would come tumbling and screeching in his direction like blood streaming from an open wound. The image made him shudder. He had been so close to laying his hands on Viola; thank the Lord he'd passed out.

Every time the shadow took hold of him, Bill found it harder and harder to resist the urge to lash out with murderous intent. Whatever, *whoever* it was, they had been a part of him since he arrived in

Hollowhills and had been pushing him towards spilling blood in its name.

Come inside…

The voice of the shadow drifted on the wind as the mournful cries of the whippoorwills in the surrounding trees beckoned the recently departed towards oblivion. The graveyard was surrounded by high walls that kept it hidden from the city dwellings beyond. Standing on tiptoes, he could make out sagging gambrel roofs and timber frame buildings with a distinctly Colonial style. He was pretty sure he wasn't even in Britain anymore. Even the trees didn't look like those native to his home.

Following the snaking path through the headstones towards the church, he felt an inexorable pull towards the entrance. Upon nearing the warped oak door, his breath stuck in his throat as it creaked slowly ajar on rusty hinges. A pale face with eyelids sewn shut in sunken sockets loomed from the darkness. The old man was dressed in a bizarre parody of Catholic vestments. The sinister regalia around his neck in place of the traditional rosary sported the unnerving eye symbol that was now seared into his memory.

"Welcome, my child," the priest croaked in a thick American accent. "Welcome to the Church of Starry Wisdom."

"Where am I?" Bill's voice quavered, betraying his fear.

"This is the Free Will Church, Providence. This is *his* church. Come inside." Sweeping his gnarled hand towards the Stygian interior, the priest stepped aside.

Bill didn't move; his feet were rooted to the spot by a deep unease that bordered on blind panic. Looking around for a means of escape, he let out a startled cry to see that the headstones were now occupied by hundreds of whippoorwills. The notorious psychopomps watched him expectantly with their beady black eyes.

"Come inside!" The priest was suddenly inches from his face, gripping his arm with his bent fingers and dragging him inside. The door slammed behind him, shutting out even the merest pinprick of light. He was strangely powerless as he was dragged down a musty corridor and thrown forcefully into the vestry. Landing on his hands and knees before a throne-like chair, he tried to muster the strength to flee.

An icy blue glow started to bloom from clumps of grotesque fungi that lined the walls of the mildewed room. A figure sat on the chair dressed in the garments of an Egyptian pharaoh. His skin was as dry as parchment and completely devoid of any pigment. He looked like a corpse. "Nice to meet you face-to-face," the figure chuckled. He was clearly amused by something.

"W-who are you?" Bill stammered.

"Come now, Bill, Billy, Will, Willy, William. It's not that simple, is it? You see, I, like you, have many names. Some call me the Crawling Chaos, some the Haunter of the Dark, the Mighty Messenger. Others have called me lord and pharaoh, and others still have called me a demon and devil. I am all of these things and none of these things. I am Nyarlathotep, and you will be my vessel."

The building creaked and shuddered at the mention of this blasphemous name. Bill shifted away from the gaze of the evil entity before him. "What do you want from me?"

Again, Nyarlathotep laughed and leaned forward, revealing for the first time a complete void where his face should have been. "You will do my bidding. You will become my mask!"

Bill screamed.

♎︎☒☖♃

Sunlight streamed through Bill's bedroom window. Still screaming, he sat bolt upright and looked around in confusion. He was fully clothed and the bedsheets were sticky with blood from his injured hand. It was undressed and untreated; thick clots had adhered it to the white sheets and they came away when he moved his arm. He had no idea how he had got there. His mind was a complete blank after screaming at Viola.

"Viola… What was I thinking?"

Filled with a penitent urge to apologise profusely and beg forgiveness, Bill rolled out of bed and stripped off his filthy garments before dressing anew and leaving his bedroom. His hands were trembling uncontrollably. His body was screaming for the earthen kiss of the laudanum. He had procured enough to keep him going for a while, but now that he and Lester had parted ways, he had no idea where he was going to get more. Still, one problem at a time. He had amends to make.

Walking along the landing, he noticed that Viola's door hung ajar. In all their time together, he had never once seen the inside of her room. Peeking through the gap, he was shocked to see the room was completely bare. Pushing the door open, he was hit by the awful realisation that Viola had gone. The one link he had to his past, to his parents, had left, and it was all his stupid fault.

"No, she-she can't have gone…" His contrition quickly morphed into self-pity as salt tears started to sting his aching eyeballs.

Hurrying downstairs, he barreled through to the kitchen and was relieved to find Susan hunched over the table kneading a lump of dough. Flour was absolutely everywhere; she had been beating it within an inch of its life. She had clearly been taking out her frustrations on it.

"Susan, where's Viola?"

His sudden appearance gave her a start. "Oh! Master Bill, thank the Lord ye have surfaced. I thought ye were a goner at one point."

"I don't understand."

"You've been out of it for two days now. I came in t'other mornin' and found you unconscious at the bottom of the stairs. As Viola had gone in the night, I 'ad to get Jack to help me carry ye up to yer room."

"Oh. Sorry." He looked sheepish for a second before confusion set in. "Gone? Why has she gone?"

"You tell me." Susan slammed her fist into the dough with such force that her knuckles tore holes in it. "You babbled that ye had got rid of her, ye did."

"What? I...I don't remember." Susan's words hit him for six. Feeling faint, he placed his hands flat on the table to steady himself. "Did she leave anything to say where she was going?"

Susan sighed. "Not a sausage. All I know is what ye told me, and ye weren't makin' a lot of sense. Ranting and raving about some old church ye were. Kept repeating a word: Nyarlathotep."

This sent his head spinning.

"Oh, my word, you don't look well." She gave the dough a reprieve from its sound pummeling and raced around the table to his aid. "Let's get ye through to the dining room and I'll rustle up some breakfast. A good solid meal will do ye the world of good." She draped his arm around her shoulder and steered him out of the kitchen. "Oh, ye definitely need a good feed. There's nothin' to ye. I've seen more meat on a chicken wing."

Sitting him down in one of the plush upholstered chairs, Susan fussed over him for a second before trotting off to the kitchen. She had been planning to give him a royal ear bashing but seeing him in a state like that brought out her maternal instincts.

Bill racked his brains trying to remember what happened after he dropped like a stone to the library floor. No matter how hard he tried, he couldn't peer through the shadows in his mind. It was beyond frustrating; he knew there had to be something there, but nothing would reveal itself.

The clattering wheels of a hansom cab passing his window broke him out of his trance. It came to a rattling stop outside of Conley House. Getting shakily to his feet, he wobbled over to the window and peered around the curtains. He was just in time to see a distinguished-looking middle-aged man with a balding pate leap down from the cab and plant both feet in a large puddle of mud. It must have been Kenneth Conley's nephew, Aiden. Bill frowned, if he knew Lester like he thought he did, that poor chap was going to be his next target. He shrugged before collapsing back into the chair. Hopefully, he would have more brains than Bill did and send him packing. If he was feeling better tomorrow, he'd go and warn him about Lester.

Once he had eaten the gargantuan plate of food Susan placed before him and located his precious laudanum, Bill took himself back to bed and slept for the remainder of the day. He awoke after nightfall and went down to the library to try to find out anything related to this Nyarlathotep character. Taking the catalogue from under a jumbled pile of bills of sale and other mine-related admin, he searched for anything that could possibly contain mention of the creature. He scoured books on Egyptology and Cotton Mather's book, but came up empty. As he scowled at the almost blank occult page, something caught his eye. It was those numbers that his grandfather had scribbled in the corner: 22, 33, 55, 11. It was the second number that got him thinking. "Thirty-three, what did Lester say? Communication."

If he was correct in his assumption, Lester was at least being truthful about one thing: his family *did* have links to the Brotherhood of the Flame. This was bad—very bad, indeed. He suddenly felt like a pawn in some kind of cosmic chess match; the flame on one side, and the shadow on the other with him in the middle being ripped in two.

Cursing, he swiped a stack of books off the desk in anger. Under them was an envelope with his name scrawled across the front in George's familiar crabbed script. As he had launched the letter opener to Lord knew where on his last visit to the library, Bill had to tear it open with his grubby fingernails. The page was smudged and the writing barely legible; George had evidently been under considerable strain when he wrote it.

Bill,

If you are reading this, then the poison I am to consume after writing this confession has worked as promised. My father kept a vial hidden in the top of his cane in case he fell into the clutches of his enemies. It was extracted from the golden dart frog and is allegedly one of the most toxic substances known to man. I guess we will see just how toxic.

I have failed you, my boy. You were right to hate me. I thought by keeping you away from that despicable man, Lester, I was keeping you safe. Sadly, I was wrong. It wasn't only the thing that he worships that you had to worry about, but the thing that lurks in this ancient and cursed place. I didn't want to leave without explaining a few things, in the hope that the knowledge will help you fight the forces that amass around you, and perhaps save your soul.

Our family and the Lesters, along with the Greens and Angoves, were the founders of the settlement that became Hollowhills. Lured by the mineral wealth under the soil, they established several mining operations and began to prosper from their plunder. Things were splendid for a couple of generations, according to my ancestor's diary, until the Green mine broke through into a system of tunnels that pre-dated the Roman occupation. That was when things started to go to hell.

According to the records, these tunnels had been not so much carved out of the rock as gouged. They ran for miles under Bodmin Moor, eventually reaching a series of natural caverns. The brave miners went down searching for gold and other treasures, but found only madness and disease. Some of them came into contact with a sticky black ooze that corrupted their flesh and warped their minds. They either died or were locked away for the good of the community. It is said that if you stand at the Edge on a moonlit night, you can hear the moans of those tormented souls.

The corruption wasn't limited to the miners, however, the crops withered, the soil soured. Cows dried up and the chickens went barren. Soon, the population of Hollowhills was starving. If that wasn't bad enough, the villagers started to vanish. Those who witnessed one man being dragged away spoke of savage creatures. Several people were afflicted with strange dreams of a bulbous creature on a black stone. These poor fools formed a church of sorts to the demon of the mine and sought to sacrifice people to keep it appeased.

Finally, the elders, our ancestor, Josiah Johnson included, got together and decided that enough was enough. They needed to deal with whatever was plaguing them, but they were going to need help. One man amongst them, Alfred Lester, was something of an explorer, much to the chagrin of his family, who preferred to wine and dine over hard work and toil. I suppose I saw something of him in your father, hence my harsh treatment of him. Yet another thing I regret.

Alfred had spent a great deal of time in the wilderness of Tibet. While there, he came into contact with a curious tribe known as the Tcho-Tcho. From them, he learned of the great old ones, an ancient race of creatures from the stars that man worshipped as gods back in Earth's infancy. This secretive group of cannibals ate members of his party as payment for imparting knowledge of the Burning One, Cthugha, to him. Once he returned he spent the best part of his family's fortune on the purchase of a library of dark grimoires and occult treatises. His family thought him a madman, but they had little choice but to give him a chance.

He took a team of stalwart chaps into the depths of the Green mine and tasked them with filling the lowest chamber with hundreds of tallow candles.

Once they were lit, he had a goat led into the chamber, slit its throat, and doused it in oil before igniting the cadaver. Only a couple of the men returned alive, the others were immolated as Alfred Lester chanted and brought forth the old one, Cthugha into our world. Those that survived were as mad as march hares and took their own lives soon after. Only Alfred returned unscathed.

For all intents and purposes, the ritual was a success. The subterranean chamber was now protected by a wall of living flame. The tunnel leading into those dreadful caverns was collapsed and the mine sealed. The Angove family moved to High Bend soon after, so the Greens took over the running of their mine. Everything was perfect—for a time.

Gradually, the Lester line used their bond with the entity, Cthugha, to take control of the village. Not content with their own wealth, they used the Burning One to usurp the Green family from their mine. Soon, the Lesters came knocking on my grandfather's door. Powerless against the might of the old ones, he agreed to a fifty-fifty share of the mine and all of its profits. This kept the Lesters happy, for a time, but my father was far from happy.

Following in Alfred Lester's footsteps, he scoured the world for forbidden books relating to the Great Old Ones, eventually finding what he was after. It seemed that the old ones, far from cooperating, had natural rivalries and were openly hostile towards each other. One such hostility was the eternal battle between Cthugha and the Crawling Chaos, Nyarlathotep. These 'outer gods' fought for the favour of their father, Azathoth, and had been locked in a pitched battle for aeons that stretched far across the cosmos. This probably sounds like the rambling of a disturbed mind. Perhaps it is, but you will by now have come to the realisation that, as mad as it seems, I speak the truth.

Using the families wealth, he procured a trinket unearthed from a crumbling Egyptian fane. It was a curious crystal that resembled a trapezohedron. It was said to be one of the conduits of the avatar of Nyarlathotep, the Haunter of the Dark, and when used correctly, could make him manifest... Oh Lord, why didn't someone stop him?

When the mine fell to my father, he called upon Nyarlathotep to banish the Brotherhood of the Flame. For thirteen days and nights, an unholy battle took place in the rabbit warren of tunnels under our feet. I was only a small boy when this occurred, but I can still hear those monstrous sounds that came from underground every time I close my eyes. Eventually, it subsided and the two foes withdrew, seemingly at a stalemate.

Unfortunately, my father's plan failed in two key respects: Firstly, neither foe left Hollowhills and are locked in an impasse somewhere in the abandoned tunnels of the forsaken Green mine. Secondly, Nyarlathotep was possibly the worst entity he could have called upon. Clearly, his knowledge of the old ones wasn't as deep as he imagined. Had it been half of what he thought, there would have been no way in hell that he would have summoned the Crawling Chaos.

Nyarlathotep has many names and hundreds of forms and avatars. It is written in the Necronomicon that "Where Nyarlathotep went, rest vanished, for the small hours were rent with the screams of nightmare." As his sobriquet would suggest, he is the agent of chaos, manipulating life from the shadows, reveling in the carnage he brings. He is the embodiment of darkness, heavy impenetrable darkness. He is also known as the Faceless God and collects people as "masks." I fear he wants us both as such. I am too old to fight, too frail to resist, I am an old man. This is why I must take my own life.

You, on the other hand, are young and fit and may have a chance to fight back. It pains me to say this, but you will need Dr. Lester's help, at least for the first part. Help him free Cthugha. Once he regains his powers, he can chase Nyarlathotep back to the audient void. Then, you must find a way to stop Lester. My hope is that without Lester's worship, Cthugha will return to his world of Fomalhaut. This is why I banished his cronies. He and Conley are the last of the brotherhood. You see, I have been working to free Hollowhills from the grip of the old ones for most of my life.

I thought that I had Nyarlathotep contained by certain wards, such as the one on the hearth. Unfortunately, your anguished mind was like a beacon to him, inviting him over the threshold. Once your blood had been spilt on the ward, that was it; it became useless. I have no remembrance of destroying it. I can only assume that I was his puppet at that point. I have been losing more and more time as he has been acting through me, as I am sure he is trying to act through you. I have done many things that I am to be damned for, as I am sure you will learn in time.

I can fight it no longer. The buzzing in my head is like ten-thousand hornets, the will of Nyarlathotep asserting control. The books that you will need are in my sanctuary. The key is in my desk drawer. Take them and learn what needs to be done. You have so little time. I can feel him getting stronger. He wants me to kill you. Stop Nyarlathotep and get out of here. Raze this accursed house to the ground. Purify it with flame.

One last thing, don't trust anyone. Nyarlathotep has eyes everywhere, whether they know it or not.

Good luck, My Boy. I am so very sorry.
Your grandfather.

P.S. Whatever you do, don't go in the attic. Only madness awaits you there.

Bill sniffed back the tears that were dropping onto the page and causing the ink to run. "I'm sorry, Grandfather, I never knew. Why didn't you tell me?" Despite his sorrow, the letter had at least removed one of the weights from his shoulders; *he* didn't kill George. But if he took his own life, why didn't the post-mortem reveal the poison? There was only one answer: the man who did the post-mortem kept it from him. "Damn you, Lester, damn you to Perdition!"

In light of his grandfather's words, Bill was now faced with a problem. He, apparently, needed Lester's help, and the last time they conversed, he had basically told the man to go to Hell. It was going to take more strength than he currently possessed to both apologise and not punch him in his lying mouth. No, he would cross that particular Rubicon after a good night's sleep. For now, he would locate the key, take a lamp, and go to retrieve the books that George mentioned.

It took a few minutes of rummaging to locate the key, after which he rose and staggered out of the library, taking his lamp with him. That was one good thing about coming from a mining family, you were never short of a safety lamp or six. Sweeping the light ahead of him to keep the shadows at bay, he slowly made his way through the kitchen and out of the back door. Despite sleeping most of the day and having a good feed, Bill was still tremendously weak. His mounting reliance on opiates and alcohol was rendering his youthful vigour down to a vapour. Though he couldn't see this fact and all he could think about was whether George kept any spirits in his shed.

Around halfway up the lawn, a startling roaring sound came from somewhere close by in the village. Bill turned and was perplexed by the orange glow that lit the night sky to the east. It danced and flickered like the tip of a candle flame. Shrugging to himself, Bill mused that it was a funny time of night to be having a bonfire and figured that Jack and Tom were on the sauce again. "Gittings will have your guts for garters, lads." He smiled and, thinking nothing more on the subject, hastened towards the shed.

George had certainly made a comfortable little nest for himself over his last few weeks on Earth. The seating had been augmented with cosy cushions and thick woolen blankets. The wooden workbench had been turned into a makeshift study. Piles of books and reams of paper covered in his grandfather's scrawl eclipsed all traces of the wood beneath. Sitting himself down, Bill started to sort through the mess. Most of it was paranoid gibberish, evidently written during his struggles with the shadow of the Crawling Chaos. The books, on the other hand, would prove useful, as would something else he found when he gathered up the tomes—a bottle of brandy.

"Bill...wake up, for God's sake!"

Opening his eyes slowly, Bill looked at the blurred outline of the female face that owned the hands that were shaking him. "Viola?" His voice was little more than a scratchy wheeze through a throat swollen through dehydration.

The tone of the woman changed from one of concern to irritation. "What the 'ell is wrong with you? Viola's gone. It's me, Kirsten."

His mouth moved but no sounds were forthcoming as his eyes tried desperately to focus despite the pain stabbing into them. He had fallen asleep face down on the table by the window.

Kirsten poured him a glass of water from the jug that Susan had given her to tip over him should he fail to respond. "'Ere, drink this."

Bill gulped thirstily, then panted for breath. "Thanks."

"Ye look bloody awful!" She sighed. "What the 'ell has 'appened to you, Will?"

"Hard to explain..."

"I haven't seen ye for weeks. What's going on around 'ere?" Kirsten through up her hands and fought back the well of hysteria that bubbled up from within. "It's so 'orrible."

The penny finally dropped and Bill realised that something was wrong. "What's wrong?"

"Oh, Bill…" Kirsten broke out in floods of tears. "They're all dead! Lester… 'e went mad, now they are all dead, except me and Jack."

"What?" Bill's jaw hit the floor. "Lester's dead?"

"Is that all you took from that?" Kirsten snapped. "The man was insane! 'E tried to raise some kind of fire devil or summat. 'E tried to burn us all. 'E killed Tom and Gittings. Aiden Conley died saving me and Jack from the fire devil. 'E'd have killed us all if Jack 'adn't stuck him with a pitchfork! I can't stay 'ere, this village is cursed. I'm getting as far away from 'ere as possible."

"W-what? You can't leave."

"I can, and I ruddy well will. I 'ad an offer of a position in Betyls Cove some weeks ago. I'm going to take it. I was 'oping that you'd come with me. There will be plenty of opportunity for a clever man like you in town." Kirsten smiled the way she used to before he went off the rails.

Bill wanted to say, "Yes, I'll come with you," but the low level thrum at the base of his head wouldn't allow it. "I-I can't…"

"Fine!" she snapped. "I'm leaving on the first coach in the morning. You 'ave until then to change your mind." She ripped open the door calling out, "Good day, William!" behind her as she marched down the stairs.

Slamming his fist into the desk, Bill cursed whatever had a hold of his tongue. He wanted to plead with Kirsten not to go, but simply couldn't. Every time he even thought about it, the buzz would intensify and pain would stab into his grey matter. Finally giving up, he poured himself a brandy and gulped it back. The warmth of the alcohol went some way towards banishing the fog from his mind. Standing and stretching, he attempted to process what Kirsten had just told him. He should have pressed for more details, but all he could think about was George's letter. How could he get Lester's help now that he was dead?

This conundrum occupied Bill's mind for most of what remained of the afternoon, after already having slept for most of the day. Finally, after consulting his grandfather's books, he decided on a course of action, but it would have to wait until nightfall.

♌︎♎︎♉︎♑︎

The night air smelled of smoke and burnt fabric. Bill stood on the doorstep and surveyed the village. It had been drizzling for most of the day so the pub benches were empty. The green was clear and the only activity was old Jack and a couple of constables from Betyls Cove poking around in the remains of the stable house and barn of Conley House. The sight of a couple of peelers was the last thing his nerves needed, considering what he planned.

Wrapping himself in his late grandfather's greatcoat, he took to his heels across the green, clinging to the shadows cast by the few sparse trees and the church spire. Due to the opium in his system, his movements were less than catlike, but he managed to get to Lester's home and around the back without being spotted by any curtain-twitching locals. They had probably had more than enough scandal and excitement after the previous evening's pandemonium.

Bill had been there enough times to know that Lester never locked his door. Slipping inside, he swiftly located a small oil lamp and struck a match. The wick sizzled and flared into life. Bill was apprehensive about carrying a naked flame around in the home of a worshipper of a fire god, but what choice did he have? It wasn't as though the darkness was without its dangers. Keeping the lamp at arms' length, he passed through the parlour and navigated his way to Lester's study.

It was funny, before the incident with the living avatar of Cthugha, Bill had never considered Lester's inner sanctum in any way disturbing. Now, however, all the paintings of geometrical shapes and symbols struck him as deeply unsettling. The one that hung over the desk was particularly unnerving. He had discovered a sketch of it in one of his grandfather's books and knew it to be the *Fomalhaut Geometry*—the symbol of the Burning One.

Sitting in Lester's wingback chair, Bill started to rifle through the vast collection of medical notes and occult scribblings looking for anything remotely related to his plight. After a while, with irritation mounting, he stood and paced the room. From certain angles, the painting behind the desk would catch the light in an unusual way. The *Fomalhaut Geometry* would flare when viewed in alignment with the oil lamp. Moving closer, he inspected the painting. The lines of the symbol had been inlaid with gold leaf, giving it a shimmering quality. Touching it with his finger, Bill gasped as it sizzled and smoked.

Pulling his finger away, he reached out with his other hand and yanked the painting off the wall and turned it to face the corner. Deprived of light, the painting became inert once more. Bill didn't have any time to puzzle over the painting as removing it had revealed a concealed safe. The heavy iron door was engraved with the same occult symbols that adorned the walls of the study.

"It must be in here," he mused as he inspected the locking dial. Though he still wasn't sure what *it* was. He was looking for anything even vaguely helpful at this point.

Close examination of the lock revealed that the lock had been specially constructed around the eleven times table. This was puzzling for a moment, but a close examination of the engravings on the safe revealed the answer. Curving around the circumference of an engraving of the *Fomalhaut Geometry* were the Latin words:

Ambitio – Communicatio – Mutatio – Proditione

"Ambition, communication, change…I have no idea what the other one is. Where have I seen this before?" Scratching his stubbly chin, he had a sudden realisation. "Of course!" Patting his pockets, he located his grandfather's notes and gave himself a mental pat on the back for having the foresight to bring them along. There, on one of the pages relating to the cult of

Cthugha, was a list of the words: Ambition, Communication, Change, and Betrayal. Each had a corresponding number. Read together these were more than familiar.

"22, 33, 55, 11. That must be it!"

The harsh metallic rasp of the dial was followed by a satisfying *click* as the lock released. Pulling the heavy door open, Bill's senses were assaulted by a pungent concoction of musty books and sulphur. Taking out the books and placing them on the desk, his hand fell upon a domed object wrapped in a piece of sackcloth. He took the item out and held it by the lamp as he uncovered it.

"Oh, dear God in Heaven!" he barked as he uncovered a charred human skull. The surface of it was riddled with scrape marks and over half of its surface had been chipped away. Bill stared in horror as the flame from the lamp suddenly flared, jumped, and settled into the eye sockets of the skull. Whimpering and gibbering, he threw the skull into the air and covered the lamp. The skull crashed to the floor and smashed into a heap of black powder.

Once he was sure that the skull was safe, he struck another match and relit the lamp. Fragments of skull drifted and twisted in the air like ashes. Bill grabbed the sackcloth and tossed it over the remains. After steadying himself with a good nip from his omnipresent brown bottle, he returned to Lester's chair and started to peruse the late doctor's journals. They provided a more detailed account of the history of that accursed village, though these were skewed to make the other families look like the evildoers and painted his ancestor in something of a heroic light. This was all interesting stuff, but Bill was looking for something more practical, so he started to skim through the dusty books. Eventually, in the most recent of the volumes, he came across something that both horrified him and gave him hope.

It was dated one day before the incident in Lester's study that set Bill against him and began:

Things are moving towards the inevitable conflict. The shadow of Nyarlathotep is growing stronger, feeding on poor Bill's troubled mind. I have done my best to prepare him bodily for the coming fight, but I am yet to finalise the link with Cthugha. Of late, I have upped his dosage of sacred ash to two grains per batch of laudanum. He has shown signs of becoming one with the fire, but the shadow is too strong and seems to block the effects.

No, I must introduce him to the Burning One…soon. Cthugha must be freed from his exile. Then, I will take my place by his side. Nyarlathotep and the rest of the Great Old Ones will fall before us.

Bill rubbed his eyes in confusion. "Sacred ash? No." He looked at the cloth on the floor covering the powdered skull. "He wouldn't have, surely?"

The diary continued after the disastrous introduction of Cthugha and confirmed a few things:

Damn that boy to the lake of Hali!

I have done everything in my power to make him a willing conduit for Cthugha's cleansing fire, but alas, he has fled like a frightened child. Perhaps I should have taken more time? Perhaps I should have revealed the truth with a daintier touch? I had no choice, curse it! The shadow is so close to consuming his soul and wearing him as a mask that I was forced to act. If Nyarlathotep takes his form, the efforts and sacrifices of the brotherhood will have all been for naught.

After everything I have done to protect him, the shadow has prevailed. Since our first meeting, I have been feeding him the sacred ash, taken from the skull of my beloved wife who gave herself to

Cthugha's pyre for the cause all those years ago. It was the only way to prepare his body. He wasn't born with the sacred blood of the brotherhood. There is one soon to arrive who carries the spark. The "little flame" is soon to arrive.

I fear I may have to take drastic actions. I seriously doubt that he'll be a willing participant.

Bill's vision blurred as he realised the truth. Ever since he lost the top of his finger, he had been ingesting fragments of the carbonised skull of Mrs. Lester. Feeling violated, he scrambled across the gloomy study, took hold of a metal wastepaper basket in both hands and proceeded to vomit for close to five minutes. Despite purging fully, he felt unclean and infected. His hatred for Dr. Lester had grown to Wagnerian proportions. He desperately craved the awful medicine, but had to fight the urge. Luckily, there happened to be a crystal decanter filled with port on one of the shelves. He pulled out the stopper and didn't bother with a glass as he tried to rid his throat of Mrs. Lester's remains.

Whether it was the effect of Cthugha or Nyarlathotep, he no longer knew, but he was filled with a desire to torch Lester's house. Sadly, that catharsis would have to wait. He still needed answers and some indication of how to stop the shadow now that the Brotherhood of the Flame was either long gone or deceased. He sighed and settled down with the port for a night of study.

♍♌♋♊

It was dawn by the time Bill finished. Lester's notes had gone on to detail his plan for Aiden Conley. He planned to use the numeric incantations, the power of mirror hours, and some good-old-fashioned subterfuge to sacrifice him to the flame and bring Cthugha through a mirror from his prison on Fomalhaut. Kirsten had filled in the blanks. Lester failed and was himself killed. Cthugha was sent back to the aether.

Further reading had indicated that the only course of action open to him now was to become one with the Burning God and hope that he would be released once his oldest enemy, Nyarlathotep, was defeated. It was a vain hope, but what other choice did he have? If George and Lester were right, the world was in grave peril from the Crawling Chaos. Unfortunately, the only way for him to do this was to consume the *sacred ash*.

Once his body was imbued with the *sacred spark,* he would have to locate the focal point for Nyarlathotep's power. Lester said that it would be a strange crystal in a black metal case. A *shining trapezohedron,* he called it. Furthermore, he said that it would be found in the attic of his home. His grandfather's words came back to haunt him: *"Whatever you do, don't go in the attic. Only madness awaits you there."*

Gathering up the ash in an old cigar box and slipping it under his coat, Bill sneaked back across the village and slipped inside unnoticed. Clattering pots and pans announced to him that Susan had arrived. He had little desire to feel her scorn over Viola's leaving, so he decided to make straight for the attic. The hatch was situated in his grandfather's room. Bill located a sturdy chair and climbed upon it. Reaching up with both hands, he cursed bitterly. The hatch was locked. With a sigh of resignation, he decided to ask Susan if she knew the location of the key.

As he made his way down to the kitchen, a thought struck him. Maybe he should just run? Maybe he should meet Kirsten and flee to Betyls Cove? Sadly, he knew deep down that it would do no good. Nyarlathotep would find a way to stop him from leaving as he always had. Only, this time, the injury might be fatal. He was pretty sure that he didn't have to be alive to be a mask.

By the time he reached the kitchen, Susan had gone out into the garden. She always liked to water the herbs and flowerbeds before the sun came up fully. He could see her over towards the top garden hefting a leaky watering can. Swiftly, he made his way outside and over to her.

"Mornin' Bill," Susan sighed without turning. She was concentrating on getting the water to the roots of a collection of multicoloured flowers with drooping petals.

"Morning, Susan. Do you happen to know where the key to the attic is?"

She moved further down the bed and began to sprinkle water on some vibrant purple flowers. "Um, I'm not sure. Try my 'ouse keys. They used to belong to Iris." She smiled slightly and inclined her head towards the drooping flowers as they bobbed in the breeze hypnotically. "I left 'em on the kitchen table."

Bill watched the flowers for a moment as they continued their dance before snapping out of it. "Um, thanks, Susan."

As Bill walked back to the house, Susan emptied the watering can, then moved over to the herbs to gather some sage for the chicken she planned on roasting later in the day. The keys were exactly where she had indicated. Bill scooped them up in his hand and puzzled over them for a moment before deciding to compare them to his own. The only anomaly was an old iron key with a star engraved on the shaft. He *knew* this was the one. The star design was the same as the one associated with Nyarlathotep.

Stopping to collect the box of ash from his coat, Bill climbed the stairs and prepared to face whatever awaited him in the attic.

♌︎♏︎♎︎♑︎

Thick motes of dust drifted out of the hatch as Bill pulled it open. Attached to it was a rickety wooden ladder that looked like it would struggle to hold the weight of a field mouse, never mind a strapping young man. Still, it wasn't that far to fall even if it did collapse. Hooking an unlit Davy lamp over his wrist, Bill climbed into the darkness above.

The air was thick and musty, but carried an almost floral scent that Bill couldn't place. There was no natural light and he could feel the shadow trying to seep into his mind. The buzz was returning to his pineal gland and whispers tickled his ears. Suddenly panicked, he fished out his box of Lucifers, struck one and lit the lamp. The light spread throughout the narrow peaked space and banished the insidious shadows to the corners.

"What the hell?" he gasped as he played the light over the room. In one corner was a mountainous pile covered with a large, heavy dust sheet. In the centre of the room was an artist's easel, similarly covered. Approaching the easel first, he removed the sheet and stared at the painting thus revealed.

From the size and shape of it, Bill deduced that it was the painting that had once hung over the mantelpiece in the dining room. It depicted a member of the Johnson family holding a shining trapezohedron. Behind him, looming over one shoulder, was the shadow of Nyarlathotep. Bill shivered. The painting of the Crawling Chaos was almost identical to the ones that he had been sketching. It was a frightful thing and it was no wonder that George stashed it away out of sight. As he stared into the dark eye sockets of his ancestor, the light caught the trapezohedron, making it shine brightly. Bill peered closer and realised that the canvas was slit in a grid over the centre of the crystal. Flipping the painting over, he was startled to see a black metal case open and affixed to the frame.

"Oh, thank the Lord for that."

Skitter...

A sound over to the right made him step away from the painting for a second. It could have been a rodent of some kind, and he should have focused on the task at hand, but now that his attention had been grabbed, he felt compelled to investigate the covered pile.

Gripping the sheet with both hands, he yanked it off the pile and stood and stared in confusion. He had uncovered a mountain of feminine attire and personal effects. As he moved the lamp over the pile, he spotted several items he knew belonged to Viola. Panic and unease were building again. He knew something horrible had happened, but couldn't put his finger on what. It was only as he glanced at the now uncovered back wall that everything clicked.

On the bare stone, in black paint, was the slogan: *"ANOTHER FLOWER FOR THE GARDEN."* To make matters worse, the handwriting was his own.

Flashes of the purple flowers Susan had been watering appeared before his eyes. They were violas and the ones with the drooping petals were irises.

"Oh, God, no…" Bill sank to his knees as his mind became alive with repressed memories. He saw himself in the library, struggling against the shadow as Viola returned with the brandy and bandages. It was the night before she left. He saw her eyes widen as he approached her with shadows in his eyes and his hands raised. He saw her dead on the floor—strangled.

"Oh, God! Viola, I'm sorry," he sobbed. Nyarlathotep had used his body to kill the person closest to him. Now he knew why George had been so shaken by Iris leaving. She had never left at all. She was buried in the garden next to Viola.

"Don't be sad, Bill, Billy, William…"

Bill nearly jumped out of his skin as a female voice broke the silence.

"They 'ad to die…they would 'ave got in the way."

Bill turned with a puzzled expression. "Susan?"

"Aye." The cook stood directly behind him, clutching a rolling pin. "Thanks for findin' the trapezohedron. I'd wondered where that old fool 'ad stashed it."

"But, I don't unders—"

Thump.

Bill cried out in pain as Susan swung the rolling pin at his head. He managed to get an arm up just in time, but the force of the blow shattered the bone. Squirming in agony, Bill fell into a pile of Viola's clothes, clutching his forearm.

Susan grinned. "Don't fight, deary, it'll be much easier if ye just let the shadow consume ye." Advancing on him with the rolling pin raised, she prepared to strike.

"Why?" Bill demanded. "What are you playing at?"

"Well…" She paused and tested the weight of the wooden bludgeon against her palm. "My family 'as been in yours for generations. We 'ave always worshipped the Crawling Chaos, so when yer grandfather renounced him, I set my mind to takin' over as custodian of the trapezohedron. Oh, and turn ye into a vessel, of course. My master said ye would be perfect." Her grin widened as shadows consumed her eyes. "Now, give yourself to the shadow!" Her voice suddenly changed into a hideous amalgamation of hers and that of Nyarlathotep.

Bill scrambled backwards and took the cigar-case from his pocket. Flipping open the lid and holding the case in his bad hand, he took a pinch of the powder, prayed, and tossed it into Susan's face.

A fireball erupted from the evil cook's face as the sacred ash met the shadow. Susan screamed and grabbed her face, dropping the rolling pin. As she moaned and wailed, blood started to seep between her fingers.

Bill edged around her, grabbing the rolling pin and taking the painting off the easel.

Susan's skull started to *crack, crunch,* and warp as her screams became an inhuman howl. The skin began to stretch and elongate, shaping itself into a huge fleshy tentacle.

Bill used the rolling pin to smash the casket off the back of the painting and turned to run just as Susan's head whipped in his direction, cracking like a whip. It caught the rolling pin and sent it slamming into the wall. Bill ducked and dived away from the fleshy appendage as it thrashed wildly around the room. The tip of it caught the lamp and sent it flying into the pile of clothing. The beast that had once been Susan howled and started to race after Bill as he dropped through the hatch.

Bill's foot snapped through one of the worm-eaten rungs, causing him to fall backwards and land flat on his back. Coughing and spluttering, he gazed up at the hatchway. By now, the oil and fire had spread, and a huge conflagration was taking hold of the attic. Smoke billowed out of the square aperture, followed by the abomination that had completely subsumed Susan.

Scrabbling to his feet as the monstrosity swung down on its head-tentacle, Bill limped for the door, but was caught in its hands. He struggled to free himself but the creature seemed to be imbued with superhuman strength. It howled in fury as it threw Bill against the door. The door shattered in a hail of wood and splinters. Bill was sent sprawling onto the landing, colliding with the balustrades that supported the railing. Several were dislodged and clattered down to the hall, but he managed not to follow them.

Pulling himself upright, he grabbed a piece of timber to defend himself with and limped for the stairs. The grotesque tentacle whipped towards him through the open door and nearly took his head off. Bill retaliated and swung the wood like a cricket bat. The creature howled as he connected with a *slap* and sent it slamming into the wall. Bill tumbled forwards from the momentum and went crashing down the stairs.

Landing hard on his injured arm at the bottom, Bill started to crawl towards the library. His leg was twisted and his ankle shattered. It had been damaged on the ladder, but his fall finished the job.

Crash!

The wall exploded around George's bedroom door as the howling beast came crashing onto the landing. It didn't stop, and tore the rail off as it plummeted down to ground level. It landed with a disgusting *splat* as the rest of Susan's bones were shattered and liquefied. The jelly-like mass of flesh jiggled and slurped towards him, lashing at him with its tentacle.

Bill yelped in alarm as the tip of its appendage took a chunk out of the wall inches from his head. Reaching the door, he pulled himself through and slammed it behind him. Turning the key in the lock, he edged over to the seating and pulled himself off the floor.

He knew he didn't have much time. The creature would make short work of the door. Taking both the cigar case and the casket containing the shining trapezohedron out of his pockets, he prepared to do what needed to be done.

As the tentacle slammed against the door, Bill tipped the remaining ash into a glass and filled it with brandy. As he raised it to his lips, he heard the heavy wheels of the coach pass the house. "I'm sorry, Kirsten. I won't be joining you," he said and knocked the disgusting concoction back.

The library door flew halfway across the room as

Nyarlathotep burst in. Bill started to shake and convulse, sparks shooting from his eyes. Nyarlathotep howled furiously and also began to tremble. With his final conscious act, Bill took the trapezohedron in his smouldering hand and roared in fury.

The flesh creature exploded in a cloud of matter and shadow as the crystal was blackened and neutralised. Nyarlathotep knew he had been defeated, so he formed himself into a bat-like shape composed of inky shadow and flew, screeching in anger, at Bill.

Before impact, Bill's body erupted in flames. As Nyarlathotep connected, his substance was consumed by Cthugha, who burst into this reality and engaged his nemesis.

As the forces of light and shadow entwined around each other, locked in mortal combat, the house was consumed by a shockwave of fire and darkness. The foundations crumbled as the ground opened up and swallowed it along with the combatants. After a while, the two foes retreated back to their respective prisons, once again reaching stalemate. Hollowhills had been purged of their influence.

♒︎♒︎♒︎♒︎♒︎

The residents of Hollowhills gathered around the smouldering crater that had been the Johnson home. Nobody claimed to have seen it happen, but it looked as though it had fallen into an old mine shaft or natural cavern. This was plausible enough for the majority. After all, the village was named after its abundance of subterranean passages. Funerals for Susan and Bill were arranged, despite no bodies being recovered.

As the Johnson line was no more, Lucas Gloyn, Kirsten's father, took control of the mine due to provisions that George had recently made in his will. It seemed that he had held out little hope for Bill's success, after all.

The area where the house had stood was filled in with rubble from the Conley stable house and grassed over. And, as life in the village tried to return to normal, somewhere underground, something ancient stirred…

♎︎♋︎♌︎♑︎

Acknowledgements

Many thanks once again to Ron and Deidre at Mannison Press for the fantastic job they've done on this book. Respectively, the finest editor and designer that I have had the privilege to work with.

Thanks to David Green, Rob Poyton, Callum Pearce, Neen Cohen, and many more for keeping me vaguely sane as the deadline loomed and I was nowhere near completion. To my ARC team…you know who you are. And to everyone who read and enjoyed *Burning Reflection*. If it hadn't been so well received, I doubt I would be writing this.

About the Author

Tim Mendees is a horror writer from Macclesfield in the North-West of England who specializes in cosmic horror and weird fiction. A lifelong fan of classic weird tales, Tim set out to bring the pulp horror of yesteryear into the 21st Century and give it a distinctly British flavour. His work has been described as the lovechild of H.P. Lovecraft and P.G. Wodehouse and is often peppered with a wry sense of humour acting as a counterpoint to the unnerving—and often disturbing—narratives. Tim has over eighty short stories and novelettes published in anthologies and magazines with publishers all over the world. He also has four published novellas with more coming soon.

When he is not arguing with the spellchecker, Tim is a goth DJ, crustacean and cephalopod enthusiast, and the presenter of a popular the web series After Hours with live video readings of his material and interviews with fellow authors. He currently lives in Brighton & Hove with his pet crab, Gerald, and an army of stuffed octopods.

Website
www.timmendeeswriter.wordpress.com

YouTube
www.tinyurl.com/timmendeesyoutube

Facebook
www.facebook.com/goatinthemachine

Also by Tim Mendees

Burning Reflection
(2020, cosmic horror)

As a child, Aiden Conley thought that his eccentric uncle was a vampire. Now that he is older, he realises that the truth behind the man's aversion to mirrors is far stranger. Madness and death dog Aiden's footsteps as he attempts to uncover the riddle behind the mirrors in this tale of cosmic horror. "Burning Reflection" by Tim Mendees is a Mannison Minibook published by Mannison Press.

The Pseudopod That Rocks the Cradle
(2021, cosmic horror)

Prepare yourself to enter the twisted mind of Tim Mendees. In these pages, you will find eighteen tales of sanity-shredding horror. Join a cast of uncanny offspring, randy butlers, disturbed poets, and other colourful characters as they face off against eldritch abominations and the insidious machinations of the Great Old Ones. "The Pseudopod That Rocks the Cradle" is a short story collection published by Mannison Press.